THE

BEST
NIGHT
OF YOUR
(PATHETIC) LIFE

THE BEST NIGHT OF YOUR (PATHETIC) LIFE

TARA ALTEBRANDO

DUTTON BOOKS
AN IMPRINT OF PENGUIN GROUP (USA) INC.

DUTTON BOOKS
A member of Penguin Group (USA) Inc.
Published by the Penguin Group
Penguin Group (USA) Inc., 375 Hudson Street, New York, New York 10014, U.S.A.
Penguin Group (Canada), 90 Eglinton Avenue East, Suite 700, Toronto, Ontario,
Canada M4P 2Y3 (a division of Pearson Penguin Canada Inc.)
Penguin Books Ltd, 80 Strand, London WC2R 0RL, England
Penguin Ireland, 25 St Stephen's Green, Dublin 2, Ireland
(a division of Penguin Books Ltd)
Penguin Group (Australia), 250 Camberwell Road, Camberwell,
Victoria 3124, Australia (a division of Pearson Australia Group Pty Ltd)
Penguin Books India Pvt Ltd, 11 Community Centre, Panchsheel Park,
New Delhi—110 017, India
Penguin Group (NZ), 67 Apollo Drive, Rosedale, Auckland 0632, New Zealand
(a division of Pearson New Zealand Ltd.)
Penguin Books (South Africa) (Pty) Ltd, 24 Sturdee Avenue,
Rosebank, Johannesburg 2196, South Africa
Penguin Books Ltd, Registered Offices: 80 Strand, London WC2R 0RL, England

The publisher does not have any control over and does not assume any responsibility
for author or third-party websites or their content.

CIP Data is available.

Published in the United States by Dutton Books,
a member of Penguin Group (USA) Inc.
345 Hudson Street, New York, New York 10014
www.penguin.com/teen

Designed by Kristin Smith
Set in Melior

Printed in USA First Edition

10 9 8 7 6 5 4 3 2 1   ISBN 978-0-525-42326-3

FOR VIOLET MAE

IT WAS EXACTLY TWELVE FORTY-FIVE WHEN WE
pulled into The Pines—the old tree-dotted parking lot
behind the football field. The sky was a sort of extreme blue
that seemed just right.

I felt extreme, too.

Extremely excited.

Extremely nervous.

I wasn't remotely *blue*, no, but I could hardly expect the
sky to change color for me. If it did, I thought red might do.

Or maybe violet, because it sounded like *violent*.

And *violate*.

I wasn't actually planning on violating any laws or people—or getting violent either—but I felt sort of all over the
place, emotionally.

Stormy.

Unpredictable.

Besides, I just couldn't think of a color that sounded like,
well, *psyched*.

Beyond belief.

Other teams' cars were parked in a sort of semicircle, fanned
out from a center car—which I assumed belonged to one of last

year's winners on account of the fact that it had an orange construction cone strapped to the roof and the infamous Scavenger Hunt Yeti—a four-foot garden statue of the Abominable Snowman—perched on the hood. He looked sort of pissed off, the Yeti, which made sense considering he was tonight's prize and had no say whatsoever over his own fate. I felt a moment of kinship with him as Patrick brought the car to a soft halt near a pine tree that had burst through the lot's cracked asphalt. For most of my life, and especially recently, I'd been feeling like I had no say in my own fate either. Like things were just happening—prom, senior week, graduation, summer, college—no matter what I did. It was enough to make *me* feel like retreating into some wooded or snowy clime, where only the most determined photographers or Mary-hunters might find me.

But here I was, and here was the Yeti with me. He certainly had the right stance for the occasion: one foot ahead of the other, as if at the starting line of a race, ready to run for his life.

I wondered, *Am I ready?*

Patrick offered up a more easily answered question: "Where should I park?"

"As close as you can get without getting blocked in," I said from the backseat, and Winter and Dez simultaneously pointed to a good spot. There was only one way in or out of The Pines, where an old chain typically hung between two rusty posts, and once we had the list in our hands we wouldn't want to waste even a second getting the hell out of there.

Patrick pulled his blue Buick LeSabre right up into the semicircle, then made a quick decision to turn the car around and *back* in before he turned off the engine.

"Excellent," I said, and when I stepped out of the car, the frantic chirping of birds in the pines surrounding us sounded almost like applause. It was like even they knew something exciting was happening. I imagined one of them looking at the LeSabre and saying, "My money's on that lot right there." Another one would nod its beaked head in agreement and say, "They've got pluck."

For no reason I could think of, the birds in my head sounded educated—vaguely British—but Patrick had a different take.

"Very Hitchcockian," he said, and I thought of the rainy afternoon a few years ago when he'd sat me down and made me watch *The Birds*, how I'd had black-and-white dreams about getting my eyes pecked out for days. "It's like they're waiting for the carnage," he added.

I just didn't see it that way. Not yet, anyway.

"Flip-flops?" I said, when Winter stepped out of the passenger seat. "You wore *flip-flops*? And a *dress*?" It was a sporty sundress cut just above the knee. But still.

Winter looked down at herself as if she weren't sure. "Yeah, so?"

"Sooooo," I said. "We're going to be racing. Other people. The clock. And you're going to be racing in a dress. And in shoes that are . . ."—I studied their rubbery pink platform, their sparkly little thongy thing—" . . . barely shoes!"

"I could run a marathon in these puppies," Winter said. "Not to worry. Besides, if you haven't noticed, we have a *car*."

"Calm down, ladies," Dez said, climbing out of the backseat himself, in attire more suitable to a night out clubbing than scavenger hunting—black skinny jeans, tight black shirt with a faux tuxedo print on the front, and Doc Marten boots. Winter's clothes I might have been able to influence, had I been there when Patrick had picked her up. But Dez was Dez and was not one to be influenced or ever, horrors, made over. I'd known him since before I could remember and, in our parents' circles anyway, he was still known as the boy who'd dressed up for Halloween as Daphne from *Scooby-Doo!* when we were in kindergarten. The story, considered a local scandal, had made national headlines—Dez had a scrapbook!—a fact that I'd always found ludicrous but telling about Oyster Point and where my friends and I fit in. Even before we'd learned how to read, we'd been misunderstood.

When Patrick got out of the car and I saw *his* scavenger hunt attire, I laughed and said, "Why don't we just quit right now?" He wore loud plaid shorts—held up with rainbow suspenders that had white-gloved hands for clasps—and his favorite T-shirt, which read simply SO SAY WE ALL and was a reference to a show I'd forgotten the name of. The shirt was, alas, tucked in.

"Oh, Patrick," I said.

"What," he said. "You don't like my ensemble?"

"Patrick, Patrick, Patrick." I smiled and noted the white sweat socks that climbed from his yellow Converse high-tops up to his knees, and wished that my best guy friend—we'd been nearly inseparable since we'd met freshman year—would try at least a little bit harder to hide his more geeky qualities on occasions like this. He was so intimidatingly smart that most people, even jerks, mostly left him alone—he'd probably tutored half of them by now—but I couldn't help but think he was inviting needless ridicule today. And he always took that sort of thing hard even though he pretended not to.

"Ridiculous day, ridiculous clothes," he declared, and he

smiled broadly. The curls of his unkempt black hair shook. I smiled and said, "Mission accomplished."

I had this thought: *God, I'm going to miss him.*

Surveying my team—my best friends way above and beyond any others—I shook my head and said, slowly, "We are one motley-ass crew."

Dez responded by putting an arm around Winter's shoulders and smiling overmuch as if for a photo and I said, "I'd make you all go home and change if there was time."

But there wasn't time and anyway Dez said, "Chill the ef out, Mary," and Winter said, "Seriously," and rolled her eyes. Patrick snapped his suspenders and winked.

Point taken.

We were lucky to be here on time at all—and that was my fault. I could not and would not tell my parents what I was doing today. Last year the hunt had ended badly—with a few seniors arrested and others suspended—and my mom, especially, had taken note. So I had had brunch at The Oyster Hut, the restaurant my parents ran down by the water; we ate there as a family every Saturday morning and any departure from that plan without a solid excuse would arouse suspicion. Patrick had picked up Winter—whose mom thought she was going to the mall then a movie then sleeping at my house—and then Dez, whose parents, like Patrick's, knew exactly what was going on today, before stopping by the restaurant to get me.

I'd tried so hard all through brunch to not seem anxious, eager, anything—repeating in my head *I am just going to the movies and sleeping over at Winter's,* again and again, trying to make a fake truth real. I needed my parents to believe it, and for Grace—my younger sister, a junior who luckily thought I wasn't cool enough to do the hunt anyway—to buy it, too. I had never lied to my parents about my whereabouts before and to say that it made for a tense brunch was an understatement. It was only after I'd escaped and arrived at The Pines that I finally felt all that tension leave my body and allowed nervous excitement of a different kind in.

This was my day, my night.

Our night.

Maybe the odds were against us winning, but we were going to have a hell of a time trying.

"Who invited Glee Club?"

I turned. It was Jake Barbone—*of course*—and there was no point in telling him, again, that we weren't in Glee Club. That, in fact, our school didn't even *have* a Glee Club. Dez and Winter were into drama. Winter and I were on the school paper. I did mock trial, and Patrick and I were in band and on the math team.

Yes, the math team.

So I knew how pathetic it would sound to clarify the Glee Club point. Anyway, the joke was old.

"Ha-ha-ha," Dez said, dripping with sarcasm.

"Yeah," Patrick said. "Real original."

"Look, guys," Barbone said to the back of some heads on the other side of his car, and they all turned.

If it were actually possible to put together a team of bigger (there is no better word) assholes I wasn't sure how one would go about doing it without having to advertise globally: ARROGANT, PRIVILEGED, MAN/BOY/JOCKS SOUGHT FOR EXCITING NEW VENTURE. ONLY CANDIDATES WITH OBVIOUS LOW SELF-ESTEEM AND FOUR+ YEARS OF EXPERIENCE HARASSING THEIR PEERS NEED APPLY. TROPHY GIRLFRIENDS WITHOUT MINDS OF THEIR OWN A PLUS.

"Oh, man," Dave Fitzpatrick, aka "Fitz," said, then he laughed. "Check out those *suspenders*!"

He shook his head and I felt a sort of sadness in my gut about how I couldn't protect Patrick, much as I wanted to. I felt some relief in the fact that he was going to Harvard come fall, provided some scholarship money came through, and I just knew it would. I imagined everyone there was geeky and hoped that Patrick would somehow ascend their ranks, be crowned their king.

"And look at Daphne," Barbone said.

The two girls on his team, Allison Feldman and Chrissie Arrington, just laughed and laughed.

"I didn't know they'd opened the hunt to transvestites."

"Pretty big word for a guy like you," Dez said. "Though you're obviously still having trouble using it properly in a sentence."

I couldn't help but laugh. It was all so ridiculous at this point. Graduation was only one week away. Why couldn't we all just go to our own corners and wait it out until the day we'd never have to see each other again? I, for one, was tired of bobbing and weaving around these idiots and was *so looking forward* to that day, to never having to see Barbone, specifically, again. Because apart from hounding us all for *years* in his Cro-Magnon way, Barbone had—to the surprise of many—gotten into Georgetown, on a football scholarship, while I had been wait-listed. When I was finally rejected, just last week, my lifelong status as an "also-ran" felt 100 percent solidified.

No Georgetown degree in Foreign Service for me. No sir.

Come fall I'd be enrolled in a similar program, also in D.C., at George Washington University—International Affairs—but the dream had been Georgetown and now that dream was Barbone's and it made my blood boil, much as I'd been trying to put on a good game face.

It didn't matter that my grades were better.

It didn't matter that the alumnus who had interviewed both of us had resigned from doing future admissions interviews when he'd been informed that Barbone had been accepted and I had not.

Barbone played football and Barbone's dad went to Georgetown and it was hard not to think he got the slot that could have been mine—*should* have been mine—for those two reasons.

And for a *third* reason: Principal Mullin had decided that it only made sense for him to recommend one student for Georgetown and so he'd dubbed Barbone alone "Georgetown material." When I had presented my case to him—pointing out my stellar grades and recent regional mock trial victory—he'd simply said, "Then how come I barely know who you are?" Feeling stung, I'd almost said, "Because you're too busy sucking up to football players," but I'd bit my tongue, hard.

It was a wonder I still had a tongue.

"I have to say"—Barbone brushed his own chest and smiled in advance of what he was about to say—"that the Yeti is going to look *pretty freaking awesome* in my dorm room next year."

He turned to Fitz but it was, of course, meant for me when he said, "The Yeti is *totally* Georgetown material." He high-fived Fitz and walked away while my face burned.

I could not move.

"Don't let him get to you," Winter said, sliding an arm around my shoulders.

"Yeah," Dez said. "He's probably going to flunk out of Georgetown anyway."

"Not helping," I managed, wiping away tears whose quickness to arrive took me by surprise.

"Come on," Patrick said, coming closer. "Don't be like that. You were so psyched for this!"

It was true.

I was.

Or had been.

And could be again.

"Guys," I said. "We *cannot* let Barbone win the Yeti."

My friends exchanged solemn looks and nods, and there were whoops and laughs coming from Barbone's general vicinity, and Patrick said, "Agreed."

"Yeah," Winter said.

"Totally," Dez said.

"Hey," Patrick said, waving to someone behind me. "There's Carson and those guys."

And pushing up through my tears I felt that excitement start to return. Because everything about Carson was exciting.

Carson and Jill had been dating for nine months, which was pretty much *forever*. Walking toward them, I felt a pang of jealousy and longing, even though I knew everything wasn't as it appeared. First there was the matter of the car they were leaning on, the Lexus hybrid SUV Carson had found waiting in the driveway on the morning of his seventeenth birthday back in January. It hadn't had a bow on it like in TV commercials, but the keys had been in a small box that was presented at the breakfast table by both of his parents, or so he had told us all, and so everyone else believed. About a week later, though, he'd slipped when talking about his parents having been out of town and the dates didn't line up right for the birthday scene he'd described. Only I had noticed.

Then there was the situation with Jill, who was still technically his girlfriend, but apparently Carson had said something to our friend Mike Bono, who'd said something to Winter, who'd then told me, that Carson wanted out.

Maybe even today.

I felt bad for Jill, of course—she was part of our circle of friends now—but I'd had a crush on Carson for years and time was tick-tocking on anything ever coming of it. Ever since he'd moved to Oyster Point two years ago and walked into my parents' restaurant with his family on the day they'd moved in, I'd felt a sort of giddy nervousness whenever he was around. Not just because he was so seriously cute but also because he seemed to know so much more than I did about the world, because he'd *seen* more of it. The giddy nervousness was, for a long time, accompanied by this idea that he was, somehow, out of my league, but I'd recently decided that I was being silly, that it was only his *parents* who were in a different league than my parents. The restaurant provided a comfortable life for us, but nothing like the luxuries that Carson's architect dad and hedge-fund-manager mother provided him. But that didn't have to dictate my fate. I could be with someone who owned skis, and went to Europe every year, and drove a Lexus hybrid SUV, and practically lived at Mohonk Mountain House, this ridiculous swanky resort a few miles from Oyster Point—even if my father didn't own a boat like Jill's did. It could work provided we loved each other. The only thing standing in the way was Jill.

Patrick and Dez had walked over to Carson with me. Winter, who'd lagged behind, finally came, too, and everyone said their hey's and hi's and how-are-you's. Carson's team was rounded out by Mike Bono and Heather Melling, who were both the sort of easy-going, up-for-anything people you'd want on your side during an enterprise like this. And their entire team was, for the record, appropriately dressed, in shorts, sneakers, and T-shirts, like I was. Carson looked totally awesome in a cool slate-gray graphic tee with a picture of a guitar on it (*of course* he played) and a pair of black cargo shorts. He had Converse on, like Patrick, but his were gray like his shirt, and both laceless and sockless. The sight of the hair on his legs made the hair on my arms stand up for reasons I didn't want to think about. I got the sense that Carson's knowledge of the world also included a fair amount of knowledge about the opposite sex. There, for sure, we were not a match.

"This is going to be so much fun," Jill said, and she pulled me into a black cloud of fruity-smelling curls, then stepped back to show her straight-toothed smile. It was all so *sweet* that I felt bad for having a thing for her boyfriend. But the thing had predated her and, also, romantic feelings were out of our control. If four years of high school and hormones had taught me anything, it was that.

"Barbone just bragged about taking the Yeti to Georgetown with him," I blurted.

"And he called me a transvestite," Dez said, shaking his head.

"Oh, Mary," Jill said, "don't let him get to you."

"That guy is such an asshole," Carson said, giving me a look that I took to indicate that he'd say more if he could. It was looks like these—looks that had become more frequent during our time together on prom committee while poring over DJ applications and catering menus—that had me convinced that Carson had finally . . . what was the phrase . . .

woken up to me, and that I was the reason he and Jill were heading for Splitsville. It was possible I was imagining it, but I wasn't imagining the way my feelings for Carson had started to intensify, the way that everything he said and did seemed to take on more meaning.

Patrick put an arm around me right then and said, "We'll take him down a few notches today, Mary. Don't give it another thought."

And for the first time, I felt strangely guilty about the Carson crush I'd never once mentioned to Patrick.

I also felt guilty about how awkward I felt having Patrick's arm around me. Though the truth was I'd been feeling weird just being around him ever since prom, which was supposed to have been a great epic night but had turned out to be, instead, an epic fail.

Dez said to the group, "We have *got* to win this thing. You guys or us, it doesn't even matter."

Carson looked at me and said, "We're gonna try our best, Shooter."

And I swooned. Because I loved it when he called me that. Outside of my family, who'd dubbed me "Shooter" when I was three years old and had sucked down an oyster shooter at the restaurant bar without batting an eye, no one else ever did.

For the record, I had orchestrated our participation in the hunt. I'd led the charge. In the past few weeks, I'd reminded everybody endlessly that the hunt, while unofficial, was part of *senior week*.

That we *were seniors*.

"I've always thought it sounded kind of lame," Patrick had said, when we'd first talked about it at lunch one day, and I'd retorted, "This, from the guy who is organizing a senior show skit about math team cheerleaders doing a cheer based on the quadratic equation?"

"Come on," he said, "that's going to be *awesome*."

He'd been chewing, then he got an idea. "Hey, how come no one's made a TV show about a high school math team?"

Winter had said, simply, "You're joking, right?" Then she'd turned to me and said, "Scav Hunt is like a bad teen comedy. One called something lame like *Scav Hunt*. I wouldn't even want to play *myself* in that movie."

But I'd laid it on thick, telling them that we were almost done with the slog that was high school and that this was our last chance to do something big together, "something worth remembering." I wasn't even sure what I'd meant at the time, but then prom had not lived up to expectations. And now that we were here it was all becoming clear: Keeping the Yeti out of Barbone's hands would definitely qualify as something big, something worth remembering.

So here we were.

"I almost forgot," I said, digging into my messenger bag, strung diagonally across my chest even though I hated what that did to my boobs. "The rules! So we're not disqualified for something stupid."

I started handing out copies to funny looks and said, "Yes, I made copies."

"Well, you're nothing if not motivated," Patrick said, taking a copy and folding it in half. The others did the same until I looked at them—all just standing there holding the rules—and said, "Well, don't just stand there . . . READ!"

OYSTER POINT HIGH
Unofficial Senior Week Scavenger Hunt
RULES OF COMPETITION

1. Forty bucks buys your team entry to the hunt, aka "The Best Night of Your Pathetic Life."

2. 3–6 peeps per team. A "Sloppy Seconds" rule allows members of teams eliminated after Round 1 (aka "losers"), or people whose performance has been deemed lacking by their original team (aka "big losers"), to jump in bed with another team (aka join said team) for Round 2 as long as that team still has no more than six peeps. If taking advantage of the Sloppy Seconds rule, you may bring one item acquired in Round 1 along as a dowry.

3. The Round 1 list (aka "Afternoon Delight") will be distributed at 1:00 P.M. in The Pines. Teams must return to The Pines by 6:00 P.M. with a minimum of 1250 points in order to obtain the Round 2 list (aka "Nighttime Is the Right Time"). If you're late, you're out. Please. No begging. No bribing. No sexual favors. Don't embarrass yourselves.

4. All items/stunts on the lists can and should be obtained/performed legally. The Yeti takes no responsibility for bail payments, legal fees, destroyed friendships, groundings, rescindment of college admissions or scholarships, lost limbs, locusts, plagues, etc.

5. We encourage you to seek sponsors and freebies whenever possible as we strive to be an equal opportunity event. You *can* spend your own money if you must but don't go broke on account of Scav Hunt. That'd be lame.

6. Sabotage, if found out, should be reported to the Yeti, who will decide whether expulsion from the hunt is in order.

7. There is a category of points called Special Points that will be awarded at the discretion of the Head Judge for Special Points. For example, if we say, "Bring us a Derek Jeter jersey," and you get it at Target, you get the measly 5 points on the list. If, however, *Derek Jeter is wearing that jersey*, you can appeal to the Head Judge of Special Points and earn anywhere from an extra 2 to 2000 points for being so gosh darn special. Nudity, when not required by item listed, will not yield Special Points. And all Special Points are awarded at judging and not a minute before.

8. The Yeti knows about Google! He's familiar with the Interwebs, enemy to the spirit of the Scavenger Hunt. Use it sparingly, perhaps to ferret out clues, but count on JPEGS being worth dick. (If we say "Bring us a *Breakfast Club* movie poster," and you bring us a printout of a JPEG photo of said poster, you get bubkes.)

9. Keep your phones on and make sure the Yeti has your numbers. Texts will announce updates, clues, and additions to the list. If your battery dies and your charger gets abducted by aliens and both P.C. Richard and RadioShack were already closed and blah-blah-blah . . . we don't want to hear it. A phone with a camera and video camera is required to participate *if you want your team to stand a chance*. All photographic evidence must be texted to the Yeti before relevant deadlines.

10. Final judging starts at 1:00 A.M., and teams not back to The Pines by then will be disqualified. BE ORGANIZED. If it takes us more than five minutes to confirm your points total, we're outta here. The Yeti has many good qualities but patience is not one of them.

11. (That's right, this list goes to eleven!) The victor takes home the Yeti, 300 bucks, and has the honor of running next year's hunt.

NEXT TO THE YETI'S RIDE STOOD LETICIA FARRICE
and the rest of last year's winning team. I didn't remember
all their names but Leticia was pretty much my idol. She
had ruled the school as last year's senior class president—a
title Winter had campaigned for this year, with me as her
reluctant VP candidate. We'd lost to "The Matts," aka Matt
Sadowski and Matt Horohoe, a loss I had mostly taken in
stride because there was a part of me that would have voted
for them, too, if I hadn't felt too dumb not voting for my own
ticket. I wasn't thrilled that losing a *vice* presidential election made me the also-ran of the Also-Rans. There was certainly no glory in being the Oyster Point High equivalent of
Joe Lieberman, especially when Principal Mullin probably
didn't have any idea who he was either.

Leticia had won her election by a landslide and had even
successfully negotiated an arrangement with Principal Mullin whereby seniors could leave school for lunch or other
free periods, a feat that had secured her legacy forever. I
had channeled her when I'd negotiated peace over the prom
committee's Battle of the Prom Song, a fierce showdown that
had pitted the pop kids against the hip-hop kids against the

indie/alternative kids. When I'd had enough (let's face it: all three songs were pretty good), I'd suggested, simply, that we have the DJ play all three of them, in a random order to be determined by drawing straws, at the high point of the night. Everyone had seemed content with that and they didn't know it but they owed it all to Leticia, whose spirit guided me. She had just finished her freshman year at Yale, and here she was, a stone's throw from me, with the Scavenger Hunt list in hand, to pass on the hunt tradition. I wanted very much this time next year to be one of the seniors who returned like this, victorious, looking exotic and worldly and *over it*.

Over high school.

Over Barbone.

Over everything.

Leticia blew a whistle quickly and loudly and people started to draw closer to her. "We need your entry fees," she shouted, and so I got out my wallet and said, "I'll go."

Carson reached for his wallet and said, "I've got this" to his own team, and I felt even surer that something was up between us, at long last, or had always been.

So we went up to pay, side by side, and Carson said, "Liking the pigtails."

Without looking at him, I smiled and said, "Thanks," and I felt like maybe asking him flat out why he hadn't broken up with Jill yet.

All week at school, since hearing the rumor that a breakup was imminent, I'd been going about my business, waiting for word of it. All week, I'd sort of avoided Carson on account of the horrible awkwardness of my raised expectations but now here we were.

Me with pigtails.

Him liking them.

"Is Winter pissed about something?" he asked and, surprised by the out of context-ness of it, I crinkled my nose and said, "I don't think so. Why?"

"No reason," he said, and I realized it was true that Winter was acting sort of subdued around Carson. Maybe she felt as awkward living with this rumor about the impending breakup as I did. Because much as I'd tried not to think about it or talk about it too much, it had been impossible to not fantasize about what life would be like once Carson was free.

To be with me.

"Hey," said a guy, who I sort of remembered from last year because he'd started a petition in school to start a paper-recycling program—something we still didn't have and which Earth-hating Mullin didn't much see the point of.

"I can take that." He pointed at my two twenties.

"Oh." I handed the cash over, and he said, "Which car?"

I pointed and said, "The blue LeSabre."

"Riding in style," he said, and I said, "Always" and smiled because he was cute, and seemed funny, and why not. He then made me text "LeSabre" to the phone he held, a phone I could only assume was the official Yeti phone.

"The rest of your team can text me, too, if they all want to get the alerts," he said, then he moved on to Carson's entry fee and number while I eyed the Yeti. I wondered how heavy it was, whether I'd be able to take one of each of those two hairy-looking feet in each hand and heft him over my head in a gesture of victory. There was no way to know.

Not yet.

"You're Mary, right?" said the judge guy, and I turned and right then his name popped into my head. "Yeah, and you're Lucas Wells?"

He smiled. "Yeah."

"The recycling guy," I added.

"That's what I'll put on my tombstone, yes," he said, and I laughed.

Then I had nothing to say and he just said, "Good luck to you," and I said, "Thanks."

"You cool?" Carson said as we walked back toward their friends.

"Why wouldn't I be?" I said lightly.

"I just mean Barbone and the Yeti-Georgetown thing." He looked genuinely concerned, his eyes a bit sad.

I said, "Let's just say I'd feel a whole lot better about it all if he didn't win the hunt."

He shook his head. "He's not smart enough to win the hunt."

"But we didn't think he was smart enough to get into Georgetown," I said. The fact of it still boggled the mind since Barbone had always behaved like he had rocks in his head. Sometimes, like during last week's senior show, when he'd done a weird reinterpretation of the famous Chris Farley "Van Down by the River" *SNL* skit—this one about Principal Mullin, living in a trailer down by the river—I swore you could hear them knocking around in there. It was true that Mullin owned an RV, and the principal himself had seemed amused, but he'd been alone in that. Barbone, while laughable at times, was not particularly funny.

"Well, we'll see what we can do," Carson said, then he put an arm around my shoulders and squeezed and he smelled so good that I thought I might die.

Leticia blew her whistle again—hard and loud and long this time—and all talking stopped. Engines that were idling switched off. A few short whoops rose up from the parking lot, like bubbles that quickly popped, and my eyes wandered over to our school in the distance, a big brick U on the hill leading out of The Pines. I imagined its bricks bulging from all the memories contained inside of it—like my own memories of long hours of practice in Mr. C's band room where it always smelled of old spit, and where Patrick and I sometimes played duets after everyone else had gone home; and of the time when the whole school got detention because someone popped the balloons on the bulletin board announcing that one of the teachers had won some big award. I remembered crying in the second floor bathroom the day I'd heard that Jason White had asked Maria Ward, and not me, to the junior prom; I remembered consoling Winter in a far corner of the library the one time she had ever had her heart broken, all the way back in sophomore year. I remembered Dez's reprise of his Daphne costume this past Halloween, when the rest of us had filled out the Scooby-Doo crew in a show of solidarity. (I'd made a pretty good Velma without much effort.) When you piled in all the memories—and those were just mine!—it seemed a wonder the whole place didn't just explode.

Leticia produced a megaphone and said, "Welcome to the ninth annual, completely unofficial, uncondoned Senior Week Scavenger Hunt."

Whistles and "yeah baby"s rose up—there was a stray, drunken sounding "You are *so hot*"—and I started feeling jittery, started shaking a leg. I looked over at Patrick and his eyes were alight. He was excited, and I was relieved. I was afraid he'd be bringing all of his sounds-dumb baggage into the day's festivities, but he seemed genuinely up for the hunt now, which would make life better for all of us.

"In my hands," Leticia Farrice continued, "I hold the first list!"

More whooping it up.

"I wish *my* name was Leticia Farrice," Winter said, and I studied Leticia's super-white teeth and brown skin and wondered for the first time what ethnicity—or ethnic*ities*— deserved credit for creating this glorious human specimen, wondered how Leticia's parents looked at their baby girl and knew she'd be just glamorous enough to pull off a name like that.

Le-TEESH-a! Fa-REES!

As opposed to a name like, well, Mary May *Gilhooley*.

I looked at my best girlfriend sideways and elbowed her. "Winter Watson is a pretty great name."

Carson had drifted forward from his own car to better hear what Leticia was saying and he snapped a finger in front of my face and said, "Pay attention, Shooter."

He was totally flirting, which I admit I probably would have thought was bad form if it wasn't me he was flirting with. Jill was *right there*.

"Yeah, *Shooter*," Patrick said, sort of obnoxiously. He'd never much liked my nickname, though he'd never been able to give me a good reason why except that I already had a name—a good one, he said—and that he didn't really like oysters at all and didn't much see the point of a food that you barely ate before swallowing, slime and all.

Either way, they were both right to snap me out of it.

It was important to pay attention.

But then Leticia put the megaphone aside and said something to her friends, then took up the megaphone again and said, "Okay, sorry. Just give us a minute." So I kept an eye on her, but also set about assessing current threat levels.

There were maybe only ten or twelve teams, and only a handful that I thought mattered.

Carson's team mattered. Because Carson was on it. But also because they were pretty good competitors. Arguably a little more daring than my own team, a fact that made me sort of sad, but what could you do.

Tom Reilly's team—the skateboarder/slackers who still managed to get decent grades—mattered because they weren't quite assholes, but weren't good kids either. So, more daring than Carson's team. Way less afraid of getting in trouble than me and my team.

It was possible The Matts—our senior class prez and VP—and their team mattered because they were jokester types and clever if not book smart.

Kerri Conlon's car of towering girls from the basketball team mattered, though it was unlikely they'd do anything to jeopardize their scholarships to places like Seton Hall and Villanova and B.U.

Anyway, I couldn't worry about any of them just yet. At least not until after the first round, when I could see who was left for the second list. So the only team to worry about right out of the gate was Barbone's. Not that there was much we could do. They'd either get 1250 to qualify or they wouldn't. But I still wanted to be sure to not lose any opportunity to know how they were doing, maybe even to foil them, though I had no idea how.

The real problem was this: I was pretty sure they would do *anything* to take home the Yeti.

Anything.

And they were the kind of kids who never got caught. Or if they did, the charges mysteriously seemed to go away. So they cruised through life acting like they had nothing to lose, an assumption I took issue with. From where I stood, they had *plenty* to lose. Cars, credit cards, iPhones, varsity letters. The real problem was that there was no one around who had the courage to take any of it away. And if none of *those* people—no parents or principals or coaches—had ever been able to take anything away from Barbone, how did I stand a chance?

Leticia Farrice said, "When I throw the lists in the air, the countdown starts. If you don't make it back here by six o'clock with twelve-hundred-and-fifty points, you're eliminated. You'll have until one a.m. for the second list *and the first list stays in play*, then we'll tally points and declare a winner. Read the rules again so you don't do something dumb."

I raised eyebrows at my team as if to say, *"See?"*

Patrick smiled and shook his head.

Leticia brought the whistle to her mouth again, blew it once fast, and then threw a stack of bright orange papers into the air. Most fell right to the ground without fanfare but a bunch more fluttered down lightly, the breeze in the air catching on the staple and opening pages up to form wings.

A sudden glimpse of my sister, off to the right of Leticia Farrice, leaning on a pine tree with a beer can in her hand, made me freeze. "My sister is here," I said, and Patrick said, "Why?" then said, "I got this," and took off to get the list.

I pulled out my phone and texted Grace: WHAT ARE YOU DOING HERE?

I looked across the parking lot as people ran for the list—snatching orange paper birds from the air—and for their cars and saw Grace pull her phone out of her pocket, then look up and around. Not finding me, she looked down again and typed. Grace had recently been "acting out," as my parents put it, and they were always talking about how to "handle her." Most recently, my mother—whom I'd started to view as some kind of mostly benevolent but slightly maniacal dictator with whom all of my interactions would be good practice for my career in diplomacy—had followed Grace and her friends down to the river, to a party she'd been forbidden to go to, and had dragged her home then grounded her for a week.

My phone buzzed.

JUST HANGING OUT.

I shot back: THIS IS FOR SENIORS

Grace shot back: REPEAT: JUST HANGING OUT. NOT DOING HUNT.

I shot back: AND DRINKING?

Grace shot back: LIKE YOU DON'T?

I looked up. Chaos everywhere. My sister had finally spotted me, and she raised her beer can, as if to toast, and then took a hearty swing. She put her beer down on the hood of a car, typed again, and the text came though: AND ANYWAY, WHAT ARE YOU GOING TO DO . . . TELL MOM?

She sure told me. Because she knew that if I got caught lying about tonight, caught doing the hunt, my parents would ground me for much longer than a week.

Patrick was fast, good thing, and skinny, and he seemed to slip right up to the papers fluttering around Leticia and then, superhero-fast, he was running back toward me, multiple copies of the list actually shoved into his suspenders. He was shouting, "Get in! Get in!"

Winter and Dez and I headed for the car—I called shotgun—and when Patrick got in and started the engine, he said, "And *you* didn't like my suspenders!"

I laughed and grabbed a list from under one of his rainbows and handed copies to Winter and Dez, answering their cries of "Gimme! Gimme!"

Patrick put the car in gear and tore out of The Pines while all the other teams wasted time doing K-turns and U-turns so we were first out of the lot, first out of the gate. I couldn't resist the urge to stick my head out my window and shout out, "Suckahs!"

Patrick rolled his eyes and said, "Focus," and I held the list up to my face and tried to read what was there, but it was suddenly like my brain couldn't function at all. All I saw was a blur of black ink on orange, like melting chocolate candy corn, because of a lump of something gooey that was forming in my throat and working its way up.

It was senior week.

I was on the Senior Week Scavenger Hunt.

Everything was ending.

Everything was beginning.

An open, mostly drank beer can flew through my window then and landed in my lap.

"What the . . . ?" I said as Barbone's car blew past us, tires screeching. Chrissie Arrington's moon-white ass cheeks hung out the window.

"You're going *down*!" Dez yelled to them from the backseat.

But as I wiped beer off my shorts and felt the cold liquid seep through to skin, I suddenly wasn't so sure. Picking my phone up off my lap, I sent a quick text to Grace that said, JUST BE CAREFUL, OKAY?

"Guys," Patrick said firmly, "you need to tell me where to go."

"Home Depot!" Dez shouted, and Winter and I both looked at him and said, "What? Why?"

"AFTERNOON DELIGHT"

- A snow globe—20
- A slice of pizza in a Ray's Pizza box—10
- A beer coaster from the Slaughtered Pig—5
- Silly Bandz—1 per
- A Burger King crown—30
- Photo of your team with an alien—30
- Take your high-tops to the skytop—50
- Origami sheep—10 per
- A two-by-four—5 per every 6 inches
- A cardboard witch Halloween decoration—15
- Any sort of music box but double points for "Raindrops Keep Falling on My Head"—40/80
- A dustpan—10
- A cupcake—5 per
- A Dixie-cup icosahedron—65
- A brick—5
- A toilet seat—10
- A paper coffee cup (extra points if there is coffee in it and it is hot)—2
- A stapler—2
- A silver bangle—10
- Jar of fireflies—3 per
- A flag—25
- A small plastic toy ambulance that goes *squee* when you poke it right—50
- A maple-leaf-shaped bottle of syrup—75
- An ice-cream scoop—10
- A French spatula—10
- Any likeness of Tigger—20

- A loon—75
- An ice-tea spoon—10
- An M&M's wrapper/bag—5
- A #1 foam finger—35
- A grass skirt—30
- A Boba Fett action figure—35
- A fettling knife—10
- Bottle of Vick's VapoRub—10
- A remote—10
- What is the Yeti's favorite band?—100 points minus 10 for each wrong guess. (Clues available if you're willing to stick your neck out.)
- Balloon animals—15 per
- A doormat that reads "Welcome to Our Home"—50
- Picture of your team with a giraffe, a gorilla, and an elephant—25 per
- A pumpkin—30
- A plastic plant—20
- Rearrange the hay in Oyster Point Park—60
- A complete set of Harry Potter books—minus 40 for being such geeks
- An ant trap—10
- An ant—75
- A famous poem laid out in magnetic words on a fridge—75
- An orchid—20
- A leaf in an autumnal color—40
- An empty bottle of shampoo—5
- A three-hole punch binder—5
- Challenge the Yeti to a game of hangman—1
- A receipt from Ben's for exactly $4.89—40
- A scratch 'n' sniff that smells like piña colada—35

- A piña colada (for comparison, of course)—35
- A BEWARE OF DOG sign—10
- A love letter to or from someone who is not on your team—50
- A bag of sand—25
- We like gazebos. A lot. Show us your own gazebo love—10 per
- Sheet music to a movie theme song of your choice—20
- A divided dinner plate—10
- A Ouija board—45
- A toy made in the U.S. of A.—35
- A children's book—20
- A self-portrait drawn with pastels—25
- Play "Twinkle, Twinkle" on a toy piano and e-mail us the video—75
- A sheet of white letter paper—25, but deductions for any wrinkles, crinkles, folds, or tears
- Minty Frikkin' Mullet Lip Balm—75
- An unopened cable bill—50
- The Yeti has caught a chill. Can you help him out?—50
- A Hello Kitty cat—30
- Sit by the dock of a bay. Or lake. We are not picky about this one—30
- A recipe for chocolate chip banana bread—5
- Homemade chocolate chip banana bread—55
- A goldfish (alive)—65
- Put your name in lights—150
- A stretched penny—50
- A stone-cold lady near the lake in the sky will amaze you with a clue—1

- A Pictionary card and paper so that you can draw for the judges for points—35
- A twelve-pack of the quicker picker upper—10
- Shuck a Mary on the half shell—100
- A watercolor painting that includes both a flower and a bird and is not painted by anyone on your team (yes, we need proof)—100
- A postcard from New Orleans—75

"A BRICK. A DUSTPAN. A TWO-BY-FOUR. A Beware of Dog sign." From his tone it was clear Dez thought we were all idiots to not have thought of Home Depot right away, too, and maybe we were, though I'd barely registered anything on the list yet because my head was in a tizzy over points and clues and Barbone and Grace and everything.

He said, "Right there, that's like sixty-five points or something. And my dad's working today. He can help us get in and out fast."

I wasn't sure it was the best plan—it certainly wasn't the most *exciting* or *extreme* plan—but Home Depot, where Dez's dad had been a manager ever since his hardware store had gone out of business, was pretty close and we could use the drive time to get to know the list and then to figure out our next move. We needed to figure out how to get to 1250 the fastest way possible. "Okay," I said. "Home Depot it is."

Patrick changed lanes and said, "Affirmative."

Dez said, "I'll make a list of everything we can get," and started to scribble on the back of one of his pages as the car drifted down Amboy Road, a winding mix of old brick houses and small strip malls, and then past the ShopRite shopping center, where my family had done our food shopping for as long as I could remember, all the way back to when I was riding in the cart being pushed by my mother.

"What else, guys?" Dez asked, and I commanded my eyes to focus on the list. "An orchid," I said.

"A toilet seat," Winter said.

"A plastic plant?" I asked.

"That's a maybe," Dez said.

"An ant trap," Winter said, and Dez wrote again. Then he said, "Mary, you start thinking about what's next after the Deep," and I said, "Excellent. On it."

"I'll help," Patrick said, stopping too short at a yellow light that I would have blown through if I'd been driving.

"Help by not driving like an old lady," I said.

"No seriously," he said, ignoring the jab.

"Okay." I skimmed the list. "Where could we get a pumpkin at this time of year? It's thirty points."

"No idea," he said. "Next."

"Put your name in lights," I said. "One hundred and fifty points."

"What does that mean?" Patrick asked.

"That's what I'm asking you," I said.

"Oh," Patrick said, and he laughed.

I laughed, too, and thought, *Good*, because it suddenly seemed possible that the hunt and the fun of it all might be enough to get me to stop feeling weird about things.

"I don't know," he said. "The marquee at the old movie theater?"

"Maybe," I said. "I guess. Sounds hard." I scanned the list again. "Photos of your team with a giraffe, a gorilla, and an elephant. Twenty-five each." As soon as I said it, I knew. "Guys," I said. "Jungle Mini-Golf."

"Too far in the other direction," Dez said. "Maybe later."

"Wait," I said, flipping back to the first page. "There's also, 'Photo of your team with an alien'."

At which point we all said, "Flying Saucers!"

Flying Saucers was the local outer space–themed greasy spoon we'd all been going to together for years.

"We should do that next," I said. "It's close, and there's that sporting goods store and party store across the street. We can get the number one foam finger and a bunch of other stuff. Like a grass skirt and a likeness of Tigger, maybe the Halloween witch."

Then my eyes fell on this: *A stone-cold lady near the lake in the sky will amaze you with a clue.*

I read it aloud and said, "What does *that* mean?"

"No idea," Patrick said.

"None here, either," Dez said.

"Beats me," Winter said, then added, "What's a Dixie-cup icosahedron?"

"An icosahedron," Patrick said, correcting her pronunciation, "is a regular polyhedron with twenty identical equilateral triangular faces, thirty edges, and twelve vertices."

"That helps," Winter said with a snort.

"You'd know one if you saw one," Patrick said, giving Winter more credit than she deserved. Winter had never once paid attention in math, opting instead to pass notes to me.

"And you can make one out of Dixie cups?" Winter asked.

"I guess so," Patrick said with a shrug. "I'm game to try."

"There is *no way* anyone on Barbone's team even knows what that is or how to even think about making one," I said happily.

"They could look it up," Patrick said.

"They won't bother," I said, feeling confident. "How many points is it?" I flipped through my list.

"Sixty-five," Dez said.

"Awesome," I said.

Patrick looked over and smiled. "Awesome indeed."

"'The Yeti has caught a chill,'" Dez read from the list. "What size clothes do you think the Yeti wears?"

"Look at you," I said. "Already all you want to do is shop."

Dez smirked and said, "I know what I bring to this team, honey, and it ain't muscle."

"I'd put it at a five T," Winter said. "Bigger than my sister. Smaller than my nephew."

I jotted down 5T in the margins of my list and said, "Best. Team. Ever."

"We should have a team name," Dez said.

"Lame," Winter said, and Dez reached over and pinched her leg.

He shrugged and said, "We could've gotten cute T-shirts made."

Winter rolled her eyes and said, "Yeah. Size XXL, for extra, extra lame."

"I know!" Patrick said. "The Sabres!" He looked at me. "You know, because we're driving a LeSabre."

Winter groaned this time, but she was smiling.

"How about The Scavengers," Dez said, and Patrick said, "Unoriginal at best."

"How about the Lame-Ohs," Winter said, and Dez said, "That is lame-oh."

"The Mighty Underdogs?" Patrick asked, and I said, "That's pretty good," but then I had a thought about the four of us and why we were all here together in the first place.

"I have it," I said, and felt a pang of sadness and a rush of adrenaline, too, when I thought again about our years together—the unrequited crushes, the waiting lists, the lost elections, the terrorizing, more.

I looked around the car and paused dramatically then said, "The Also-Rans."

"Also lame," Winter said, after a beat, and I knew there was maybe a part of her that wondered why she hadn't risen higher on the high school food chain. She was pretty, smart— even perky when she wanted to be—and yet she opted to hang around with us instead of going out for cheer or soccer and taking advantage of the social status that would afford her. Sometimes I felt like we bogged her down, and like she felt it, too.

"*I'm* not an also-ran," Patrick said, baffled, as Dez said, "The Also-Rans," trying it on for size. And as the car took the bump into the Home Depot parking lot, Dez looked at me and said, "It's perfect, Mary." He reached forward and squeezed my shoulder and said, "The Also-Rans for the win!"

"Hit me," Mr. Mahady said when we ran through the doors of the Deep, and Dez started to show his dad his shopping list; and his dad started giving him aisle numbers, which Dez jotted down superfast. I watched with a sort of envy as Mr. Mahady took off his hat and scratched his balding head, then put his cap back on and blurted out another aisle number. There was a connection between Dez and his dad—this semiplump, balding, and pasty old dude—that almost made me want to cry; and I suddenly imagined them as teammates on some game show, like *$25,000 Pyramid* or *Win It in a Minute*, capturing the hearts of Americans far and wide.

To say that my parents would not be helping my team with the hunt was an understatement. Whether or not my mother would still let me sleep under their roof if I came out as gay was another question that always sprang to mind when I saw either of Dez's folks. Not that Dez had ever come out to me, or to any of us, mind you. Not officially, anyway. But we all just sort of *knew*—and knew that he knew we knew—and also knew that it didn't matter to us.

"Okay, people." Dez snapped his fingers. "Here are your assignments." And he started giving out items and aisle numbers and then we were all off and running through the store.

Toilet seat, ant trap, Beware of Dog, I repeated so as not to forget my assignment.

Toilet seat, ant trap, Beware of Dog

We were going to leave Home Depot with almost 200 points, possibly even more, in less than ten minutes, and I was giddy about it.

I had already grabbed a toilet seat when I headed for aisle six—SIGNS—and found the BEWARE OF DOG ones. I took one off the peg and put it down on the floor with the toilet seat then took all the other BEWARE OF DOG signs off the peg and hid them across the aisle, under a stack of boxes of gold doorknobs. I bent to pick up my loot.

"You look really cute today," Patrick said, and I turned.

I stood up with my stuff. "You know I hate that word."

Patrick just laughed and said, "Well then you shouldn't be wearing pigtails." He was holding a dustpan and a two-by-four that was about four feet long.

"So is that a universal thing?" I asked. *"Guys and pigtails?"*

"I can only speak for myself." Patrick shrugged. "Why? Who else likes your pigtails?"

I stiffened and averted my eyes. "No one. I mean, just in general I'm wondering."

I ran off in search of an ant trap and he followed, clearing his throat. I was rounding a corner when he said, "I *will* say one thing. You did not look at all cute on prom night."

And I stopped and turned.

We stood there for a moment and the gap in conversation felt uncomfortably large, a canyon big enough to swallow us both. "I don't want to talk about prom, Patrick," I said. In fact, I didn't even want to *think about* prom. I took off again, walking so fast that my calves started to burn and then taking off into a run.

Prom had been—despite my best efforts at committee meetings—an "Under the Sea" theme on account of Oyster Point's proximity to the water and its seafaring history. Which just seem so uninspired. In the end, however, it felt like the perfect theme because there were many moments that night when I didn't think I'd mind if the whole of the senior class, the whole of the town—everything except for select family and friends—got swallowed up into some crevice in the ocean's bottom. Like when I saw Barbone ripping down this gorgeous tissue-paper sort of coral arrangement so he could try to stuff his shirt so it looked like he had breasts. And when Becky Hudson actually pointed and laughed at Debbie Norton, a shy nerdy girl whose date was rumored to be her cousin, when she spilled punch on her ivory dress.

Winter had happily gone with Dez when an actual date had eluded her—and him—and none of us had thought for a second that there was anything weird about that. Then Patrick asked me and since my own prospects of a real date weren't great, either, I'd said yes. I'd been sad about it for a while, but then I finally decided that it must be a very small percentage of people in the world who go to their high school prom with someone they're in love with.

At least I *liked* Patrick.

Loved him, too. As a friend.

Though I'd never said it.

But then we'd danced that fateful dance. It was a slow song I hated. I knew Patrick hated it, too, but my brilliant theme-song compromise had opened the door for some pretty awful music and that was life.

He had looked cute that night; handsome, really, in his rented tux. And he smelled good, too, and I knew I also smelled good and looked as good as it was possible for me to look. I'd worked at it. And he'd confirmed it when he held me so close and tight, and I felt his chest inhale me. Then right by my ear, he'd said, "You look incredible," and then I'd felt his exhale, and felt it.

It.

In his pants.

And he looked at me and saw my horror.

Was that what it was?

He didn't pull away at first but then he did and we kept on dancing, but by that point I was looking over his shoulder to where Carson was dancing with Winter and Jill was dancing with Dez. I felt awkward and jealous and wanted to be in on the partner-swapping so that I could escape Patrick's embrace and dance with Carson, too. We'd worked so hard for this night, he and I—interviewing DJs as if the gig they were up for was no less important than the end of the world—and so it seemed like we should share at least one dance.

But then the song ended and we all left the dance floor and since Patrick was my best guy friend I figured the whole thing would be something we would both just silently file under "Stuff Happens" or "Penises Do the Strangest Things."

And never speak of again.

"We're going to have to talk about it eventually." Patrick had caught up with me in the pesticide aisle and his face had taken on a soft glow, like a lava lamp. I wasn't sure whether it was from embarrassment or exertion.

"But it was just one of those things," I said, still racing down an aisle. "I mean, it didn't mean anything, so there's nothing to talk about!"

"Well," Patrick said, slowing down as I did, having found the ant traps, but then Dez called to us from down the aisle. "Guys! Come on!"

He was holding a brick and a doormat that said, WELCOME TO OUR HOME.

So I grabbed any old ant trap and rushed past Patrick and his two-by-four (oh, God, he was sporting wood!) and found Dez and Winter—she was holding a plastic plant and an orchid—by the registers. Mr. Mahady ushered us through the self checkout, putting his credit card down to pay and saying, "Think of it as team sponsorship."

Dez said, "Thanks, Dad. And, if other teams come in . . ."

Mr. Mahady nodded. "I will send them on a wild-goose chase."

Dez's eyes lit up as he started to push our cart out toward the exit and I dearly hoped we would win, not just for my own sake but also for Dez's. If anybody deserved a victory lap as high school came to an end, Dez did.

We ran like bullets to the car and loaded the stuff into the trunk—Patrick and I had a quick fight about how best to handle the two-by-four, a fight that I won—and when we all got in and closed the doors, Dez shouted, "Wait." Then he ran off toward the garden center down the parking lot a ways and snapped a picture of a small white gazebo.

"Awesome," I said, when he got back into the car.

As soon as he closed his door, though, he said, "Aw, crap."

"What?" I asked, but then I saw.

Barbone's car had just rolled into the parking lot. It had been pimped out with a large stuffed Tigger, who was somehow tied to the front bumper; there was a twelve-pack of Bounty paper towels strapped to the roof rack; and an American flag flew from the antenna. I looked up the point values as fast as I could. "They've got twenty, ten, and twenty-five."

"Fifty-five points before they even hit the Deep," Patrick said. "And that's just what we can see. And we totally could've gotten paper towels just now."

"Stinks," Winter said.

"How did they even get that stuff so fast?" I asked, then didn't wait for an answer. "Well, so what," I said. "So we'll get another fifty-five while they're here."

"And it'll take them twice as long for sure," Patrick said. "Just to find the stuff."

"*Easily* twice as long," I said, but I felt sick and disappointed that my team and Barbone's had had the same impulse so early in the day. But as we headed toward the parking lot exit, I watched through the back window as Barbone's team approached the store, and saw Mr. Mahady appear with two security guards at his side.

"Hold up," I said, and Patrick braked.

Words were exchanged. Hands gesticulated wildly. Then

Barbone's gang turned around and went back to their car, with Fitz flipping Mr. Mahady the bird on the way.

"Go, go, go!" I said, and Patrick hit the gas and off we went, out onto Richmond Avenue, heading for Flying Saucers in search of aliens.

"What do you think just happened?" I asked, unbelievingly—it was almost too good to be true—and Dez dialed his dad's phone. After a minute, Dez said, "What just happened, Dad?"

He listened for a second then said, "I have never loved you more than I do right now," and hung up.

"Well?" I said, wishing Patrick would drive faster, that there weren't so many lights, and that we weren't hitting so many red ones.

"Apparently, there was an unfortunate incident with some bags of fertilizer and until they're cleaned up my dad's not letting anyone in the store because the stuff is toxic, wink-wink."

I squealed.

Winter said, "Awesome."

Patrick said, "Brilliant," and hit the gas with a bit more verve when the light turned green.

After a minute, Dez said, "I honestly never thought having a father who worked at Home Depot would be a good thing," and then we were all cracking up and Patrick caught my eye and we both smiled. And as I watched the gas stations and bagel shops and dry cleaners I'd frequented all my life fly by I hoped that that little conversation in the aisle at Home Depot had been the last of its kind.

Winter's phone buzzed. She had a text and I saw it light up on the seat beside her. "The Yeti?" I asked, reaching for my own phone.

"No," she said, then she sent a text and held her phone in her hand while she looked out the window.

"Who are you texting?" I asked, because everyone Winter usually texted was here in the car.

She said, "Carson wanted to know where we are," without looking at me.

It was weird that he'd texted Winter and not Patrick, but then again he knew Patrick was driving. But why hadn't he texted me? Because he didn't want to be too obvious?

"What did you write back?" I asked.

"I wrote Home Depot," she said flatly.

"Where are *they*?" I asked.

"I didn't ask," Winter said, and I shook my head and said, "Do I have to do everything?" and I turned and grabbed her phone out of her hand and typed, WHERE ARE YOU GUYS?

"Give me my phone," Winter said, reaching, but I held it forward toward the LeSabre's dash, so she couldn't grab it.

A second later, the phone buzzed and the text said, THIS IS JILL. JUNGLE GOLF. SO FUN!

"Well?" Patrick asked.

"That was Jill," I reported, wishing so hard that she was out of the picture and that I was texting Carson for a better reason, on my own phone. "She said they're at Jungle Golf."

"*Jill* answered?" Winter asked

"Well, Carson's driving," I said. It wasn't that hard to figure out.

"Can I *please* have my phone," she said, and I complied, and she looked at it and scrolled for a minute, then looked out the window again.

Whatever, Winter!

"So what are we going to do *after* Flying Saucers?" I said, and pulled out my list.

"I thought there'd be head shaving," Dez said randomly.

"Or eyebrows," Winter said.

"I would never shave my eyebrows," I decided on the spot, and Patrick said, "Never?" He was stopped at a red light again, so looked over at me. "Like if your life depended on it? If world peace was at stake?"

"Okay, maybe if world peace were at stake," I said with mock annoyance. Because you could never just say anything flip with Patrick around. He always wanted to know *why* you felt a certain way, what you *meant*. It could be exhausting.

"What if the hunt came down to you and Barbone?" Winter asked.

"Yeah," Dez said. "Because we've been given the impression that there isn't anything you wouldn't do tonight, to keep the Yeti from going to Georgetown."

I pictured it: my face without eyebrows. It wouldn't be pretty, no, but it would be worth it if it meant the Yeti would be coming to George Washington with me instead. I said, "Well, I guess if it came down to me and Barbone, I could live with an eyebrow pencil for a while."

"Would you eat bugs?" Dez asked.

"Absolutely," I said, puzzling again over that lady by the lake in the sky on the list.

"*You'd* eat insects," Winter said skeptically.

"If it was the only way to win, yes." I was trying to figure out when and how we could manage to catch an ant with our trap and keep it alive until Round 2.

"I don't believe you." Winter shook her head. "I've seen you jump into a pool fully clothed just to get away from a bee."

"I was hot!" I protested.

The jar of fireflies would have to be gathered at exactly

the right time of day, which was when, exactly? When *did* fireflies come out? And for how long?

"Yeah, right," Winter said.

"Would you let Barbone slip you some tongue?" Dez pressed.

"Gross!" I said, thinking more about where to get some 5T clothes for the Yeti; maybe at the sporting goods store? "And anyway that would never be on the list."

Patrick said, "I totally thought there'd be skinny-dipping." And then as the conversation went on, he kept saying it.

Again and again.

"I really thought there'd be skinny-skipping."

"I bet there's going to be skinny-dipping."

Finally I said, "What's with you and skinny-dipping?"

"Patrick just wants to see the two of you naked," Dez said, and I choked a little in my throat from surprise—Winter, too—though really I shouldn't have.

Ask a stupid question. . . .

But the truth was, for someone who'd never even had sex, Patrick had a funny kind of weirdly strong sexuality—or was it sensuality?—about him.

What if it *had* meant something?

"Maybe it's *you* I want to see naked, Dez," Patrick said jovially. "Did you ever think of that?"

"Patrick, Patrick, Patrick," Dez said, shaking his head and looking far away out the window. "If you only knew."

"Focus, people," Winter said, and so I obeyed and looked at the list. "I'm pretty sure there's a silver bangle at my great-aunt Eleanor's house," I blurted.

"And a flag."

I turned a page.

"And a snow globe."

And kept scanning.

"And a bunch of the kitchen utensils."

And scanned some more.

"And a music box that plays 'Raindrops Keep Falling on My Head.'"

I stopped talking as the point values piled up in my head.

"Guys," I said, feeling my pulse quicken, "Eleanor's house is a *gold mine*." I couldn't get words out fast enough. "She's got all sorts of old random weird crap. Probably more stuff I'm not even thinking of. Possibly like, I don't know, three hundred points worth of crap."

"We're going to take stuff from a dead woman?" Winter asked.

"Can we even get in?" Dez asked.

"Yes and yes," I said. "Keys under Mary on the Half Shell."

"Wait." Dez flipped through his list. "There's a Mary on the Half Shell on here."

"What? Where?" I flipped, too, and confirmed it—*Shuck a Mary on the half shell*—and my hands started to shake with nerves and excitement. Then Dez said, "What the hell is a Mary on the Half Shell?"

I could count the Marys on the Half Shell I knew of in Oyster Point on one hand and was suddenly sick with fear that another team had gotten to Eleanor's before us. Her house was on a pretty busy street, but the garden had grown over with weeds, so hopefully anyone who knew it was there in the first place had forgotten about it.

"Patrick, drive," I said. "Before anyone else gets it."

He made a U-turn and Winter said, "What about Flying Saucers?"

"What's a Mary on the Half Shell?" Dez all but screamed.

"It's a statue of the Virgin Mary," I explained. "In a grotto that's sort of shaped like a shell, I guess. So if we have to shuck one, it means we have to take the statue from her shell."

Dez shook his head and said, "You Catholics are weird."

"It's worth a hundred points," I said again. "That's an awful lot. And if somebody else takes Eleanor's statue, my family is never going to get over it."

We rode on in silence until a text from the Yeti came through that said, HIT US WITH YOUR EARLY POINTS TOTALS SO WE CAN SHARE. WE WON'T NAME NAMES.

So I texted in 285—Home Depot plus Mary—which wasn't exact *yet*, but we'd be there and beyond soon enough. A few minutes later a text came back that said: LEADING TEAM HAS 285.

"Guys," I said, "I think we're in the lead."

There were high fives and whoops and I could feel my heart swell just the tiniest bit but then shrink back down to an even smaller size on account of Mary on the Half Shell.

Please, God, let her still be there, I thought, and then Patrick blew through a yellow light and I loved him for it.

4

I HAD TO DIG THROUGH WEEDS AND BRAMBLE,
swatting away bugs I'd startled—God, I hated bugs—before
I could exhale.

Mary was still there.

She was maybe two feet tall, dressed in the Holy Mother's
standard-issue white-and-blue hooded robe—with her hands
pressed flat together in prayer. Her lips were tiny and pink
and her nostrils mere indents the same color as her peach
skin. Her blue eyes appeared to have been crying paint thin-
ner, since a trail of dissolved paint ran down each cheek.
Gray bird gunk soiled her gown's hood and right shoulder
and the expression on her face seemed calm, like she'd just
been waiting for me.

"I'm going to have to clean her up a bit," I said as I grabbed
her and the house keys.

"You're *incredibly* lucky no one else got to her," Patrick
said, and I knew he was right.

The way everyone in my family treated that statue—making the sign of the cross whenever they walked past it, even
just when driving by the house—had always made me a little bit scared of it, like it held some special power. I'd been

posed in front of it for pictures I was too little to remember taking, like at my baptism and my first communion. And I'd spent hours of my youth tending the weeds around her, or fighting with Grace about which one of us was going to do it. All because Great-Aunt Eleanor had brought the statue home from Italy at the end of World War Two, having purchased it in Sienna on the day victory had been declared in Europe, aka "VE-Day." We weren't supposed to worship idols as Catholics, but my family had obviously missed that catechism lesson or thought the VE-Day angle bought them a pass in this one case. Throughout my childhood, I'd occasionally prayed to the statue myself, but I prayed less and less the older I got. Not because I felt my prayers had gone unanswered—though they mostly had—but because my own pleas had become so petty, at least when you put them into words.

Please, God, can you make him like me?

Please, God, just one more cup size?

Please, God, Georgetown!

Please, God, shut me up!

Up the porch steps we went and then I fussed with the door and we all went inside, where it smelled strongly of old lady—like dust and cheap shampoo and old sock–drawer potpourri. Despite my family's best efforts, we still hadn't entirely emptied the house. Bags and bags of trash and recycling had already been hauled out, but there was just *so much stuff.*

"Okay," I said, setting Mary down by the kitchen sink, and pulling out some cleaning products.

"You really don't feel bad taking stuff from a dead woman?" Winter asked, and I said, "She won't know the difference."

"I don't know, Mare," Winter said, eyeing Eleanor's doll collection, an army of small porcelain girls wearing clothing meant to represent their home nations, like some kind of bizarro Miss Universe pageant. "I wouldn't put it past her."

"She *was* sort of scary," Dez said as he started rummaging through kitchen drawers. I'd given everybody assignments in the car the way Dez had done for the Deep.

"Well, I liked her," Patrick said, and he took the steps two at a time, heading for the upstairs bedrooms.

That makes one of us, I thought, but I didn't say it, I just set about cleaning up Mary. "Ten minutes and we're out of here," I said, and shouts came back from different rooms to say, "Okay!"

Great-Aunt Eleanor had died that past fall and I hadn't been that sad about it initially, a fact that had me sort of worried about my character. I wondered whether it was just because she had been very old and very sick and also just not that nice of a person on account of her sharp tongue and rigid ideas. Patrick agreed that it was probably because she was so old but he put a better spin on it, taking it as a sign of some kind of emotional maturity on my part.

"Well, we're all going to die," he'd said. "And when you're as old as Eleanor, it's not that tragic so that's why you're not upset."

I think he was giving me more credit than I deserved but I went with it.

For a while, anyway.

But then Eleanor, who'd served in the army as a nurse during World War II, had gone and gotten buried at Arlington National Cemetery. She'd retired with the impressive rank (especially for a woman) of lieutenant colonel and so had been given star treatment as her bodily remains were ushered to their final resting place. A band. A firing guard. A 21-gun salute. Even horses that pulled the caisson down to the gravesite.

I hadn't cried at all during the wake and the funeral in Oyster Point, but Arlington was an entirely different story. My mother had designated me as the person to accept the flag during the service. So I had been assigned a certain folding chair to sit on, on a small patch of Astroturf laid on the ground by the hole for the casket, and after six soldiers folded up the coffin flag into a tight triangle, one soldier— barely older than I was—kneeled in front of me and looked right at me with eyes deeper than seemed right and handed me the flag, reciting some speech about "a grateful nation."

I'd lost it.

Completely.

I didn't even know why.

Except that the whole thing had made me feel small and selfish and alone.

I'd gone and toured Georgetown's campus the next day— my parents hadn't wanted to travel down to D.C. twice, so we'd scrambled to make arrangements for college visits— and I'd fallen in love with D.C. and the Georgetown campus and everything and anything I heard about the bachelor's of science degree in Foreign Service—an undergrad program that prepared people for lives of diplomacy and humanitarian work across the globe. I hadn't even known that such a degree existed, but it suddenly seemed possible that I could do something that would change the world, maybe be an ambassador or work for the UN. I wasn't cut out for war, no.

But maybe I was cut out for diplomacy? I could make my life, my self, bigger—the way Eleanor had. When my parents told me, some months later, that Eleanor had left me enough money to pay for my entire college education that had sealed the deal.

"She lived quite a life, your aunt," Patrick had said one day that winter, after I'd told him he could have the old cameras of Eleanor's that he'd found when we'd first started trying to clean out the house. Long after I thought he'd gone home that day, I'd found him out front with an old Polaroid, photographing Mary on the Half Shell in the snow. The photos were instantly old looking and cool—a little bit white-washed and blurry, like the Mary statue wasn't really a figure carved out of stone but was some sort of unearthly apparition.

"She was ahead of her time," he said, and his breath was fog. "Getting her own mortgage. Getting her degree through the GI bill. Going for a master's on top of nursing. Most women back then were barefoot and pregnant in the kitchen."

I laughed and pulled my hood up and said, "You have a funny way of looking at things. And you know *way more* about my great-aunt Eleanor than you are required to know as my friend."

He shrugged inside his red parka. "I just listened to the eulogy is all."

"Well, she was certainly driven," I admitted, blowing on my frigid hands. "And she didn't really seem to like men much, so barefoot and pregnant in the kitchen wasn't likely." Eleanor had never had a kind word for her father—a great-grandfather I'd never met—who apparently drank too much.

"You're a lot like her, you know." Patrick was taking another photo.

"I like men!" I protested.

He was amused and shaking his head. "Calm yourself, Mare. I just mean that you're really driven. And independent. And focused."

"All right, Harvard," I had said, because really, who was the driven one?

"I just don't think there's anything you can't do if you put your mind to it," he said.

And for a while, anyway, at least until I'd been rejected by Georgetown, it had felt true.

"I found a silver bangle," Winter called out from one bedroom.

"I've got a flag," Dez said.

"Is it folded into a triangle?" I called back. "In a wooden box?"

"No," Dez said. "It's on a six-inch plastic pole."

"Perfect!" I said. Because I would not mess with the Arlington flag, not for a measly 25 points.

"Hey, check these out," said Dez, coming into the room and holding up two folksy black dolls with x's for eyes. "Creepy shit."

"They're handmade in Appalachia," I said, a little bit defensively. I actually wasn't sure whether the dolls were somehow racially offensive or not, and I crossed the room to take them from Dez and put them back on the shelf in the living room. Most of the knickknacks remained because there was the lingering question of whether they were worth something and whether anyone would buy them at a garage sale or on eBay. There were bells made in Mexico and shamrocked vases from Ireland, small wooden gondolas from Italy, tiny silk slippers from China.

Seriously. Was there any place the woman hadn't been?

"The three-hole punch binder is in the closet in the second bedroom down the hall," I said as a way to try to get us all moving again. "And I'm pretty sure there's a snow globe in a box in the credenza with some Christmassy stuff."

"I'll get the binder," Winter said, and Dez headed for the credenza after mockingly saying, "I'll check the *credenza*."

"What?" I laughed. "That's what she called it."

"Bingo," Dez said, and he shook the tiny half-sphere and set it on the dining room table where we watched white flakes settle slowly around an old version of the New York City skyline, one with the Twin Towers set behind Lady Liberty. Something about the towers there, towers I couldn't remember ever seeing, though there were pictures, made me feel small like I had at Arlington, too. Small enough to climb into that tiny globe and catch snowflakes with my tiny tongue.

"I never want to get old," Winter said, sinking into a couch hidden under a teddy bear collection.

"Beats the alternative," I said. Because that's what my parents always said.

Winter was waving the tiny American flag absentmindedly. "Sometimes," she said, "but not always."

An awful mix of tinny music had begun to cascade down the house's main staircase. Patrick was up there and had apparently found Eleanor's music box collection. Amid the cacophony I heard a sort of "Jingle Bells"/"Rock-a-Bye Baby" mash-up and I headed upstairs for more treasure, feeling hotter and sweatier now that the idea of Christmas had flashed through my brain.

"You're avoiding me," Patrick said, from his position in the middle of the floor in the sewing room. He was surrounded by music boxes, most of which had, blessedly, stopped playing. He picked one up then—a small yellow piano with butterflies and dandelions on it—wound it, and "Raindrops Keep Falling on My Head" started playing in earnest.

I forced a sort of *Ha* sound from my throat. "How could I be avoiding you? We've been together for"—I looked at my phone—"an hour."

"You know what I'm talking about." He started looking through a box of sheet music then, presumably for a show tune. "Not today, but this week. I mean, I've barely seen you since prom."

I felt caught out; I'd actually found myself ducking around corners in school all week, avoiding Carson and Jill, yes, but also Patrick. I wasn't proud. And maybe it was the music but I felt, suddenly, full of rainy-day melancholy.

I said, "Well, I'm here now," and sat down on the brown carpet facing him. "You want to talk about prom, let's talk."

He handed me half the sheet music pile, and I started to flip.

"Here's how I see it," Patrick said, putting his sheet music stack down. "We're going away in a few months. And I've realized that I want to be with you during that time. I mean, really be with you."

I froze.

It was the moment I'd been dreading without ever realizing I'd been dreading it because I never thought it would happen. We were pals, Patrick and me.

Buds.

Super close ones, but still.

"Here's how *I* see it," I said, my voice vibrating like I was being physically shaken. "It seems sort of dumb to start something now, when we might mess up what we already have."

But that came out wrong. It implied that I would consider the idea.

Which I wouldn't. I was in awe of Patrick, yes, but it was not the right kind of awe. Like whenever I went to church and listened to the folk band Patrick played in—which was awesome, like sixties rock for Mass—I had to work hard to not look at him because it pained me to see how intense he looked. I wondered, every time, whether that was what it felt like when you had a kid and he or she had a recital or a speaking part in a play and it all went horribly wrong and right at the same time. When you wanted to just cry out of pride and embarrassment all at once. I felt a million emotions around Patrick, pretty much on a daily basis, but I'd simply never had the urge to touch his face or hold his hand. I'd never felt desire.

"But I'm saying we've already started it." Patrick's voice seemed a little shaky, too, and when I looked up she saw that his eyes also seemed to vibrate with intensity. "I feel it."

It had to be said. No pussyfooting.

"I don't think I do," I said sadly.

"But why not?" he pleaded.

"I don't know." I sighed and thought, *I wish I did!*

"I just don't." I put down the sheet music. "We're wasting time here."

"That's what I'm trying to tell you." He came closer.

"No," I said. "I mean, with the sheet music. It's not worth enough points to spend all this time looking for it."

He hadn't stopped coming closer.

"Patrick, come on," I said. "Let's just forget about prom, okay?"

"I don't want to forget," he said.

And then I wondered what sort of stuff *I* didn't want to forget, then wondered how much of *any of this* I would remember in the end. Like if I lived to be as old as Eleanor. I sort of hoped that I'd forget most of what I'd already experienced of life. Not because it was so *bad*, but because it was so *ordinary*. I hadn't ever left the country, or made love, or gotten married, or skydived. Not that I was sure I ever *would* skydive but if I did—if life presented the opportunity and motivation—I hoped I'd remember that when I was old—the feeling of flying, of free-falling, of total liberation—and not this awkward conversation with a boy who was once my best friend. I wanted to remember Italy and Paris, rip cords and parachutes. Love, too. Even loss.

But not this.

Because right then, Patrick leaned in, like he was going to kiss me, and I turned away.

I thought about how he wouldn't even *want* to kiss me if he knew how I felt about Carson. Then thought about *telling* him how I felt about Carson for that very reason. It seemed cruel.

"You guys having any luck?" Dez said from the hall, then he poked his head into the room.

"Patrick found the music box," I said, "but we're striking out on movie sheet music."

"Wait," Patrick said. "I got one." He pulled out sheet music for "The Rose," from the movie by the same name, starring Bette Midler, and handed it to me.

Winter called out, "We should get moving, Team Lame-Oh! I boxed up the loot that's down here."

Patrick picked up the "Raindrops" music box and threw me an I'll-deal-with-you-later sort of look, and we hurried downstairs and out the door.

We left with a silver bangle [10], an ice-tea spoon [10], a stapler [2], the snow globe [20], the music box [80], the sheet music [20], the flag [25], a yellow leaf (silk, but still) [40], a remote [10], a three-hole punch binder [5], an ice-cream scoop [10], a bottle of shampoo (to be emptied later since we ran out of time) [5], a divided dinner plate [10], a stack of Dixie cups (for Patrick's icosahedron attempt) [potential for 65], an unopened cable bill [50], a recipe for Chocolate Chip Banana Bread [5], and a cleaned-up Mary, shucked from her Half Shell [100].

For a whopping total of 402 actual points.

Which, when added to the Home Depot loot, meant 587.

Like taking candy from a baby.

I locked up behind us and pocketed the keys, which I'd put back later, along with Mary.

"Isn't your mom going to be mad?" Patrick asked, then. "About the statue?"

I adjusted a few weeds as we left, so that the grotto was obscured from sight again. "They'll never know she was gone and if they do, they'll never know it was me."

Then I turned and headed for the car and saw Tigger and Bounty and Stars and Stripes.

Barbone again.

"What are you, following us?" Dez said as the car pulled in and idled at the curb.

Barbone just looked out from the driver's seat, across Fitz in the passenger seat, and said, "As if there weren't enough virgins on your team already."

Of course Barbone knew the statue was there, weeds and all. We'd all been stuck in this town a long time. But did he have to know I was a virgin? I just looked at my friends and said, "Let's go, guys."

"Didn't appreciate your dad dicking us around, Daphne," Fitz said.

"Yeah, well," Dez said. "Them's the breaks."

And Barbone's car took off with a grunt.

"Where to?" I asked after we'd loaded in all our stuff and gotten back in the car, this time with Dez riding shotgun.

"My house?" Winter said, beside me in the backseat, then she accidentally kicked Mary, who was by our feet, so I picked her up and moved her to the little shelf behind our headrests.

"Houses are boring," Dez said.

"Houses are easy," Winter said. "But we'd have to sneak in through my window since my mom thinks I'm at the movies." This was probably wise, but the truth was Winter's mother barely noticed her when they were in the same room.

"Lamest. Team. Ever," Dez said, then he started to flip through the list.

"I'm heading for Flying Saucers," Patrick said, "unless anyone's got any better ideas."

"Let's talk through some of the list," I said, pulling mine out but then taking a minute to text Winter: PATRICK TRIED TO KISS ME.

"Seriously. My house is a no-brainer," Winter said, looking up from her list in the backseat. "But we should go later tonight, I think, so the goldfish doesn't die before final judging."

Her phone lit up (she'd obviously finally had the good sense to silence it) and she read, then looked over at me, wide-eyed.

"You have a goldfish?" Patrick asked.

A text from the Yeti said: CHRISTMAS ORNAMENT FROM TIFFANY, 25 POINTS, and I wrote it onto the master and said, "Sucks."

Winter was typing.

"What sucks?" Dez said. "Did Eleanor have a Tiffany ornament?"

My phone lit up again, with Winter saying: YOU SHOULD GO FOR IT!

Looking askance at her I said, "No but my parents totally have one, but there's no way I could get it." Then I started to type: BUT I LIKE CARSON! HELLO! I hit send.

"No, my sister has one," Winter said, still holding her phone.

There were way too many conversations in the car right now, bouncing around like Ping-Pong balls.

"You're going to steal your sister's goldfish?" Patrick asked.

And, for the record, Winter's sister was named neither Autumn, nor Summer, nor Spring, but Poppy. She was all of four years old and Winter was basically raising her.

"I sure as hell am," Winter said.

I turned to her with a broad smile, while she typed. "I am so proud of you!"

"You're proud that she wants to steal her sister's gold-fish?" Patrick asked.

"I admire her commitment to the cause to claim the Yeti is all." I looked out the window to hide the *jeez* in my eyes. I had never said it out loud to anyone but I got the distinct impression that Patrick didn't entirely approve of my choice of a female best friend. He had never said it out loud either, but he didn't have to.

Winter's text to me this time said: BUT HE IS STILL WITH JILL. AND AFTER THAT, NO GUARANTEE.

I looked at her, mystified, then started typing.

"I'll buy her a new one." Winter shook her head in Patrick's general direction then started ticking off items on her fingers. "So my house has the goldfish, a Ouija board, children's books, and probably a toy made in the U.S. That's, like, seventy-five points, I think. Oh, and Pictionary. I can get a Pictionary card."

"Excellent," I said, and sent the text that said, HAPPY TO TAKE MY CHANCES.

I had to concentrate. "We should pick up a jar or bottle somewhere so when it's dusk we're ready to catch fireflies."

Winter read my text and shrugged, and I thought about the last time I'd caught fireflies, how I'd been with Patrick. And now that I recalled that night, maybe I should've known that a moment like the one in Eleanor's house was coming, and maybe had been for a long time.

THERE WERE NO ALIENS OUTSIDE THE FLYING
Saucers diner so we had to go in if we were going to take a
photograph with an extraterrestrial. Standing in the shade
made by the off-kilter spherical building—designed to look
like a UFO that crash-landed in the parking lot—I said, "I
guess we just walk in acting casual and ask some random
person to take our picture, then leave?"

Patrick shook his head. "But we don't want to tip anyone
off to the fact that the hunt is underway."

It was true that if the owners of Flying Saucers saw a
parade of kids coming in and taking pictures and leaving,
the gig would be up for sure. They'd call the cops and there'd
be cruisers out all over town and the whole thing would
eventually get shut down before the victor was named. But I
didn't see any way around that. "What else are we supposed
to do?" I asked.

"We could eat something fast," Dez said. "I'm sort of
hungry."

I said, "Tick-tock, Dez!"

"We just have to do it," Winter said. "We're wasting time."

"But there's a host who stands right at the front," Patrick
said.

Clearly, he was trying to be difficult.

"We're here all the time, so it's probably someone who has seen us before," I said, "so we'll be like 'hey, can we grab a booth' and just saunter by."

"All right, Mary," Patrick said. "Since you seem pretty committed to this plan of yours, I guess we'll just do it your way."

"A little early in the day to get snippy," Winter said, and I was grateful she said it and not me. When Patrick was in a mood, frankly, no one wanted to be around him. Winter had once put it thusly: "He's like some tortured superhero. Emotion Man."

"We're going to get in trouble," Patrick said, and we all turned. "Just stating that for the record."

"Duly noted," Dez said, then he turned to me and smiled and said, "Take us to your leader."

I headed for the front doors, feeling a tinge of nausea in my gut. Because it was possible we *would* get in trouble, but we weren't going to win if we were worried about . . . what, exactly? Losing our diner rights? They couldn't exactly call the cops and arrest us for trespassing. It was a *diner*. And if we couldn't do this—something so dumb, really—even at the risk of outing the hunt, well then it was true that we were the lamest scav hunt team ever, which maybe seemed inevitable since we were the good kids, or so everybody always said.

But I wasn't *that* good. Not if you really knew me. Like if you read my mind. Or looked at my web browser history. Or saw straight into my heart the way Patrick sometimes seemed to.

Inside, the diner was maybe half full and I scanned the room for aliens that would photograph well. The host was on the phone at the front podium and nodded acknowledgment, and I whispered, "We'll grab a booth?" and pointed. He nodded and took four menus off his stack and handed them to me and I said, "Thanks."

So far, so good.

I headed for the diner's most photogenic alien, a classic green creature with a pointy head and domelike eyes, painted on the wall near the restrooms, and found a couple at a booth who looked sort of cool, so I went right to them and the girl said, "Oh, we already ordered."

Confused for a second I said, "Oh, I don't work here," then asked, "Can you take our picture by that alien?"

They exchanged a look and a smile, and I said, "Like really quickly." I turned to my friends and said: "Guys, line up."

So they did, and I handed my phone to the guy, who seemed friendlier than the girl, and he held it up and said "smile" and then, "You might want to check it."

It was fine. Nothing special but it was us. And an alien.

Thirty points. For a total of 617.

"Thanks," I said, and my friends were already on their way back toward the door. I felt sort of revved up and strangely guilty, probably on account of my good girl shackles, and hoped that the guilt, at least, would go away the second we got past the host, who was still on the phone. I put the menus back on his stack and said, "Something came up!" and we bolted out the door and blew past Kerri Conlon's team of Amazons—who were heading into the diner all too leisurely, if you asked me—and hopped in the car.

Dez said, "Did you see how confused he was?" and laughed, but I felt sort of bad about it. Then we drove out of the parking lot and down the road about fifty feet to the strip mall on the other side of the street, where Carson's car sat in front of the sporting goods store.

"I'll do sporting goods," I said, not sure the others had even noticed his car. "Who's with me?"

Dez said, "I'll come."

So Dez and I went one way and Patrick and Winter headed for Party Burg, and as soon as we got inside I walked right up to the desk and asked, "Do you sell those foam finger things that say number one?"

The clerk, a middle-aged Indian man, looked up and said, "In the back. Fan section."

"There's a '*fan section*,'" Dez said, wide-eyed and smiling. "This is going to be good."

We walked deep into the store, past whole aisles of basketballs and soccer balls and hockey sticks and then a big lineup of exercise equipment, like elliptical machines and treadmills and stationary bikes and Pilates machines. All the while I was looking for Carson.

"Is this the tenth circle of hell?" Dez asked, and I just laughed.

Finally, on the far side of a handful of racks of New York sports team jerseys, I saw a sign on the wall that said FOR THE FANS and headed for it. Dez split off to a different FOR THE FANS aisle as I combed my chosen aisle. He soon appeared around the corner wearing a hat that had beer can holders and tubes running down to the face and also wagging a #1 foam finger on his right hand.

"Go, Mary! Go, Mary!" he chanted, then he said, "Who am I?" And continued his "Go Mary!"s.

"Quit it," I said, and Dez took off the hat with his free hand and put it on the nearest shelf and said, "I'm Patrick. Get it?"

"Don't be mean," I said.

"I'm not the one being mean," he said. There was an implication there that I did not like at all.

"You think I'm *mean* to him?"

This was the most I had ever spoken to Dez about Patrick for sure. Mostly we talk about school and music and television and movies and getting the hell out of Oyster Point. He shrugged and looked simultaneously like he was uncomfortable and enjoying having me on the hook.

"Maybe mean isn't the right word," he said. "Maybe . . . *insensitive*?"

I shot him a look.

He said, "I heard."

"Heard what?" How long had Dez been out in the hall at Eleanor's? "Heard me remind Patrick that we're *just friends*?"

"He's madly in love with you," Dez said, and I didn't want to believe it—that what I took for deep friendship, Patrick had, all this time, thought was something else—so I said, "Don't be ridiculous."

Dez raised his eyebrows in a *what-can-I-tell-ya?* sort of way.

"Come on," I said, shoving my left hand into the foam finger and poking Dez with it. "We need clothes for the Yeti, then we're outta here."

I headed back to the clothing section we'd passed when we'd come in—there was no way Carson was in this store, unless he was actually hiding from us—and Dez was right on my heels, saying, "So that's all you're going to say about it?"

Finding the children's clothes I grabbed a random hoodie in size 5T then walked back to the cashier, thinking I'd pay cash and just save the receipt and return the stuff tomorrow.

"I don't know what else to say. I just don't feel that way about him." I was suddenly a little annoyed at having to explain myself. Which was probably why I blurted, "I like someone else anyway."

"You do?" Dez asked. "Do tell!"

"Carson," I said, and Dez said, "Oh, don't join that club, honey. *Please.*"

Which was not the sort of response I was expecting, and it made me even a little bit more annoyed. I said, "What would you know about it anyway? I mean, relationship advice? Really?"

Which wasn't supposed to be as mean as it sounded, but it sure sounded mean. Because Dez had never actually dated anyone. Not that I knew of, at least.

Dez seemed unfazed, though, and said only, "Just don't get your heart broken."

Which didn't make sense, really, because I was ostensibly breaking Patrick's heart, and Carson was about to break Jill's. And anyway what if I couldn't help it? What if hearts sometimes had to get broken? What if that was just the way of the world?

I paid and we stopped at the car, which was unlocked, and put the bag (85 points, which brought us up to 702) in the front seat, and soon we were rushing through the aisles of Party Burg—"I mean, even Party *Burb* would have been better," I said, and Dez laughed—looking for Patrick and Winter, and since Carson's car was still in the lot I was looking for him and his team, too. Right as Dez and I split up, I found Patrick down an aisle full of Tiki torches and summer party supplies. He was wearing a grass skirt and looking through a bin of off-season sale items, probably hoping for a Halloween witch.

I said, "Aloha!" and he said, "Aloha," and he looked happy right then, and I hoped the whole incident at Eleanor's would just get bundled up with the incident at prom and drift away from us throughout the day, like a small iceberg. More than anything, I wanted to hit some kind of rewind button on our relationship, and go back to some point before today, before prom, before anything went wrong. The thought that all this stuff was coming up now—when Patrick and I were so close to having to move away and drift apart anyway—was just too depressing. What kind of last summer would this last summer be if we weren't back to being thick as thieves?

He said, "I decided I'm going to give you some time to let the idea sink in a bit. Then we can talk more later."

The arrogance! I thought. As if I didn't know my own heart.

But for the sake of peace, for the sake of the hunt, I said, "Fine. We'll talk later."

He nodded and I said, "What else do we need?"

He looked at his list. "Winter's getting Tigger so if you could maybe try to for a piña colada scratch 'n' sniff, that'd be excellent. And we have no idea what a Hello Kitty Cat means exactly, but maybe we should get some Hello Kitty stuff in case we come across a cat later?"

So I took off in search of stickers and Hello Kitty and heard Patrick say, "Carson and those guys are here, by the way," and felt a sort of skip in my heart, until I rounded a corner and saw a wall of Dora and Diego decorations and then Carson and Winter, talking close, and I saw the way she looked at him and bit her lip and pulled a strand of hair from the back of her neck forward and twirled it on a finger—things I knew were signs she was crushing—before she turned and walked away from him, away from me. I stepped back around the corner and found myself face-to-face with the weirdly misshapen head of Ariel, the Little Mermaid, and her sidekick, Flounder, such a strangely happy-looking fish. I thought about prom and all the backstabbing I'd witnessed in the four years leading up to it. And how until I'd seen her twirling her hair a minute ago, until I'd replayed that partner-swapping slow dance in my head, noting the way Winter had looked maybe a bit too happy in Carson's arms, it had never occurred to me that my best friend might be holding a knife behind *me*.

"What did you mean?" I asked Dez, when he appeared holding some Tigger napkins. "When you said, 'Don't join that club'?"

Dez seemed to squirm a little and for a second he studied the wall of Rapunzels to his right, as if she could save him by letting down her hair and pulling him up into some lofty tower. He said, "I just mean a lot of people like Carson. And if Patrick knew you were one of them . . ."

"A lot of people like who?" I asked, and he sighed and said, "You wouldn't be asking if you hadn't already figured it out."

So she *did* like him, and she *had* kept it from me. She'd let me go on and on about how I liked him for years and had never said a word?

"Did you see the Yeti's text?" Winter said, coming into view at the end of the aisle, and since I hadn't, I took out my phone. I was thinking was how nervy she had been in the car, trying to discourage my own crush to make way for hers.

The text said: BONUS FAST-ROUND ITEM: SEND US A PICTURE OF A BIRD, ANY BIRD, WITHIN THE NEXT FIVE MINUTES. TWENTY POINTS.

"Not worth it," Dez said. "Unless there's a pigeon in the parking lot."

"Or Tweety Bird?" I said. "Here in the store?"

We all headed off in different directions to look for Tweety Bird, and I bumped right into Carson near some stickers and took one of the same sheets of scratch 'n' sniff cocktails he was holding off the display. "Hey there," I said, feeling that nervous giddiness as I looked at those fierce eyes of his, those hands, the way the guitar T-shirt hugged his chest.

"Hey yourself," he said, and it felt flirty. But he'd looked flirty with Winter, too. Was there something a little bit flirty about everything he did?

"How's it going?" I said, suddenly at a loss for anything he and I could actually talk about, anything other than secrets. Did he *know* that Winter liked him? What would happen if I told him? Besides her killing me. Was that what they'd been talking about?

"Okay," he said. "I guess."

But he looked distressed and I imagined, for a second, that it was from the pressure of Winter's unwanted advances. If he was going to break up with Jill to be with me, the last thing he needed was my best girlfriend crushing on him. I thought about saying something, like "So that's weird about Winter, huh?" or "Don't worry about Winter, I'll handle it," but here, in Party Burg, with everyone else just an aisle or two away, it didn't seem wise; and maybe there was a part of me that was still scared of sticking my neck out.

I didn't know for sure that he liked me.

Even an hour ago, I'd felt certain our paths were about to collide in a big, romantic way, but now . . . ? The story I'd written in my head about how this was all going to go down didn't seem to be lining up with reality. Winter at the very least—Patrick, too—had thrown away my script. How was I to know Carson wouldn't, too?

When Patrick appeared and said, "I sent a picture of Tweety Bird and grabbed some Hello Kitty stickers in case you hadn't found them," I was grateful for an escape from the paralysis of the moment. I headed his way, but then Carson said, "Mary?" and I turned.

"Do you think cheating is ever justifiable?"

At first this seemed entirely out of the blue to me but then it started to make sense. But I didn't want him to *cheat on* Jill. I wanted him to break up with her. And cheating was one thing I felt really strong about.

Really anti.

"I don't think it's justifiable," I said. "No."

I wanted to scream, *Just break up with her, you idiot!* I said, "Cheaters are cowards."

"Yeah," he said, nodding quickly. "That's what I figured you'd say." Then he walked off and I met Patrick and the others at the registers and I worked to hide my confusion. What on earth was Carson thinking? That we'd have an *affair*? It was ludicrous.

Dez counted points while the cashier rang up our items, including thirty Silly Bandz and a pack of M&M's we grabbed by the register. "One forty," he said. "Which brings us to eight forty-two."

"Awesome," I said, ticking things off on our list. "Crap! Balloons for balloon animals."

"There's no way we're going to find time to sit and learn how to do that," Patrick said.

"Let's just go," Winter said.

Another text from the Yeti said: BTW, RUMOR HAS IT ONE TEAM JUST HIT 750. WILL YOU BE FIRST TO QUALIFY? REMEMBER, POINTS ABOVE 1250 STILL COUNT IN THE END!

"Lake in the sky," Dez muttered as we headed for the car. *"Lake in the sky."*

"What about 'Challenge the Yeti to a game of hangman'?" I said, with my own list in hand, noting that Carson's car was gone. "What does that mean? And why is it only one point?"

Winter said, "Maybe it means we're supposed to challenge the Yeti to a game of hangman."

"But how?" I said, and rolled my eyes.

"Text him," Patrick said.

So I did: WANT TO PLAY HANGMAN?

"Lake in the sky," Dez said again.

I asked Patrick: "Jungle Golf? Or Winter's house?"

"Either," he said.

"Another house is lame," Dez said, the last word in a high-pitched, two-syllable singsong, then he took out his phone and typed something into it as Patrick started the engine with me riding shotgun again.

Patrick said, "Jungle Golf'll be a quick stop. I mean, we won't actually golf, right?"

"Right," I said, and got this text from the Yeti:_ _ _ _ _ _ _ _

I said, "Looks like we're playing hangman with the Yeti." Which made our total 843.

"Awesome," Patrick said.

"Hold up," Dez said, from the backseat.

Patrick was about to turn in the direction of the jungle animal photo op.

"*Mohonk* means lake in the sky."

"We're supposed to go all the way to *Mohonk Mountain House*?" Winter said.

I knew what she meant, but the truth was Mohonk wasn't that far, it just felt that way because it was so unbelievably expensive that neither of our families could ever afford to go there. The only person we knew who'd ever been there over-night—not just to visit the grounds or to apply for a catering job, like me—was Carson, whose family had reunions there every summer.

"Hold on." I set my phone aside after texting the letter *E* to the Yeti and looked at the list.

Things started to click.

"I think there's a *bunch* of Mohonk stuff here," I said. "There's gazebos and a maze made of shrubs and a dock there."

"The lady will a*maze* you," Dez said. "There's probably a clue hidden in the maze."

"Should we do it?" Patrick asked.

NOPE, the Yeti said.

I sent in the letter *A* and got this back:

_ _ _ _ _ _ _ A

The highway entrance was right there. I sent in the letter *O*.

I asked, "How many points are we talking?"

Dez did some quick figuring and said, "Probably only a hundred or so, depending on how many gazebos there are. Plus the clue."

_ O _ _ _ _ _ A

"I think we should do it," I said, shooting in the letters *S* and *T*, with no luck, then *L*.

Patrick said, "It's probably going to take us an hour and fifteen total to get there, do the stuff, and get back." The drive was probably twenty minutes each way. It was already—I looked at the clock on my phone—ten to three.

How the hell had that happened?

We'd be back by four, four thirty.

My phone lit up: _ O _ _ _ L L A

Gorilla! I thought, and I sent in *G* to be sure.

"I think it might be worth it," I said, "because there's no way to know how important the clue is, right?"

What came back: G O _ _ _ L L A

But I tried Gorilla. It didn't fit.

"What's another word that sounds like gorilla?" I said. "G. O. Blank. Blank. Blank. L. L. A."

"I need to see it," Patrick said.

I held the phone out and he looked and I said, "And if not a lot of people figure it out or do it, that may give us a real advantage. I mean, I seriously doubt Barbone's going to go all the way to Mohonk. It just doesn't seem their speed at all. And I'm pretty sure someone at Mohonk would see their car all pimped up with Tigger and kick them out or something."

Winter laughed and I was sort of irritated by the sound of it. Since *when* did she like Carson? What had she and Carson been talking about in Party Burg? And why had he cozied up to me so much during prom committee meetings? Was it because I was Winter's best friend and confidante? What if none of it ever had anything to do with me at all?

"I need directions, people," Patrick said with a little too much edge, I thought.

"Just head north on the highway," I said. "There are signs."

He had handed my phone back to me while we'd been talking and I said, "Well?"

He said, "Godzilla."

"Of course!" I said, and I sent it in.

The text I got in return said: WELL DONE.

"That's it?" I said. "The Yeti just said well done. No points, no nothing."

"Mysterious," Patrick said.

"Annoying," Dez said.

POINTS? I texted.

The Yeti wrote back: NOPE.

CLUE? I wrote.

And the reply was: TOINSNW CLRUILHCH

"Okay," I said, "Now it looks like we've got a word jumble."

Dez asked to see my phone so he could look at the clue and after a while he handed my phone back and the photo with the alien was on the screen. "Why were you looking at this?" I asked. "Is it okay?" Because if we had somehow screwed it up, it was better to know now.

"Yeah," Dez said. "It's fine. It's just, I look at it and I sort of see two aliens, if you know what I mean."

"You're not an alien, Dez." I wanted to hug him.

"Well, no, not here. Not with you guys." He rested his head back on the headrest. "But at school I am. And at college, who knows? College is another planet."

"A better planet," I said, because he was going to school in the city, and we all thought of New York as a better place. "You'll fit right in."

I believed it. I had to. Because I was counting on it being true for me, too.

"Don't suppose you can do a word jumble if I just read you the letters," I said to Patrick, who shook his head, but there was plenty of time to figure it out once we got to Mohonk.

Right?

The next text from the Yeti came through on all our phones a few minutes later and said, SEND ME VIDEO OF YOU RINGING THE BELL IN FRONT OF FORT WAYNE AND I WILL REWARD YOU AN ADDITIONAL 50 POINTS. OFFER IS GOOD FOR THE NEXT TWENTY MINUTES ONLY.

80

"Get off here!" Winter shouted, and Patrick said, "What? Why?"

An exit was rapidly approaching and Winter explained, "We're only like five minutes from Fort Wayne and there's fifty points on the line there for the next twenty minutes."

"Crap," Patrick said.

He was all the way over in the left lane. Traffic was brisk.

"We're going to miss it!" Winter shouted.

"Winter," I said, "are you sure this is the right exit?"

"Yes," she insisted. "I'm sure. Hurry, you'll miss it!"

"Dude," Dez said, looking out the back window. "Go now. After this white car."

"Everybody calm the heck down!" Patrick yelled, and then he looked over his shoulder and checked his mirrors, pulled into the middle lane, and then did it again, into the right—a shrill *beeeeeeeep* came from the car he cut off—and then he went off onto the exit ramp. We all seemed to breathe a sigh of relief, then, until Patrick said, "Now which way?"

I started trying to load Google Maps on my phone.

"Make a left," Winter said, "and then a right at the third light."

"Oh, that's right," I said, and turned to Winter. "I forgot."

"Forgot what?" Patrick asked.

"Forgot that Winter loves men in uniform."

"I do not," she said.

Fort Wayne was a military academy and because one of Winter's cousins went there, she'd been invited to a dance once and that had turned into more and more invitations.

I started singing, *"I love a man/ I love a man/ I love a man in a uniform,"* and Winter pinched me on the shoulder hard and said, "Stop it. I don't."

"But you do!" I said.

"I don't!" Winter shouted, and I just said, "Okay. Jeez. Sorry."

"I think maybe Winter has a secret boyfriend she's not telling us about," Patrick said, entirely unaware of how close he was to the truth. "I mean, a right at the third light? When have you ever known Winter to know how to get *anywhere*?"

"I don't have a secret boyfriend," Winter said.

"She doth protest too much!" Patrick said, and Winter just shook her head and looked out her window; and we were all quiet until we arrived at the gates to Fort Wayne, where I heard the deep clang of a large old bell even before Tom Reilly and his team came into view. We parked next to their yellow Volkswagen Beetle with its bumper covered in stickers for weird skateboard and surfing brand names I'd never really heard of. We got out and went over to talk to them. But I quickly realized I'd left my phone in the car and went back for it. I saw Winter's phone just sitting there, too, and I did a pretty awful thing. I woke it up and read a text from Carson that said, WELL SHE WON'T BE MY GIRL-FRIEND FOR LONG.

I felt like I froze from fingertip to toe, but apparently I didn't because I had it in me to scroll back to read: HOW WOULD YOUR GIRLFRIEND FEEL ABOUT THAT?

And before that, Carson's text that said: WISH I WAS ON YOUR TEAM.

These next few things happened as if in slow motion.

I put the phone back.

I noticed my hand trembling.

I got out of the car and walked across the parking lot.

I rejoined my team and planted a smile on my face while I wondered whether anyone could sense the way my skin felt like it wanted to jump off my body, run screaming from me.

My friends were talking to Tom Reilly and Steve Paglia, who was cute in a way I'd always found sort of foreign and alarming—he was just too perfect—and for a minute I wondered why I hadn't ever nurtured or pursued *that* crush, instead of letting Carson overshadow other possible boyfriends. It suddenly seemed like I'd made all the wrong choices because here I was, about to graduate, and I'd never really had a boyfriend at all. Worse, I was after the same guy that my best friend was after and it was *her* he was making promises to, *her* he wanted. Whatever signals I thought I'd been reading—*liking the pigtails*—I'd been reading all wrong.

"How many points do you have?" Tom asked Patrick, who said, "I don't even know, man, but a lot. I mean, we'll qualify for sure."

"Yeah," Tom said. "I think we will, too."

"What about Barbone?" I asked Steve, feeling like someone else must have taken control of my body in order to get those words out. "Have you seen them?"

"Nah," Steve said, and something about the way he looked at me—never actually making eye contact, but looking in the general area of my forehead—made me realize he had no idea who I was.

Four long hard years and I hadn't even registered.

Looking to Patrick, who apparently *had* registered, Steve said, "We saw Kerri Conlon and those guys leaving Flying Saucers when we were going in but that's all."

Their other teammates were already back in the Volkswagen and they drove over and Steve said, "Let's roll."

So they drove off and we sprang into action—my body still on autopilot, behaving as if it weren't breaking from the inside out.

We went up to the bell. Patrick reached for the rope that hung from the ringer and he rang it three times while I filmed him and then sent the video in to the Yeti for 50 points. Which meant we were at 893. The others all headed for the car, then, but I felt the whole thing was sort of anticlimactic, with only Patrick doing the ringing, so I went for the bell and rang it myself, loud, wanting more than ever to be *noticed*.

By Steve Paglia.

By Carson.

By Mullin.

Anyone!

"Jesus, Mary," Winter said, jolting on her walk back to the car. "A little warning would have been nice."

I said, "Oh, you're one to talk."

When she looked at me funny, I said, "What's going on with you and Carson?"

She blinked three times fast. "It's complicated, Mary." Then she took off toward the car and to the sanctuary Dez and Patrick would provide.

"All right!" Dez declared. "Mohonk awaits!"

So we got back on the highway and settled in for the twenty-minute drive with Dez softly singing "The Rose"—"*I say love/it is a flower/and you its only seed.*"

"Those can't be the words," Winter said, sounding almost annoyed.

"That's what it says." Dez held up the sheet music.

Winter just shook her head, and I put my sunglasses on and sank back into my seat and told my skin to calm the ef down. I thought I should probably forget about Carson and Winter and just tally all our points—double-check everything to be sure going to Mohonk wasn't a huge mistake—but I thought for sure I wouldn't be able to read through the tears forming in my eyes. Because this wasn't how it was all supposed to go, or how it was all supposed to end, and I wondered, Was this what it was going to feel like when we all had to say good-bye come fall?, and then wondered about good-byes in general, and how anyone ever survived them at all.

MOHONK MOUNTAIN HOUSE LOOKED LIKE IT
belonged somewhere else entirely, like in the Swiss Alps or
the hills of Germany, with all those balconies and turreted
towers, and all those rich people lurking behind the hundreds of windows. We parked in the visitors' lot and went
to get day passes in the admissions office after a quick fight
about whether it was possible to "break in" to Mohonk,
and whether we should try. Then we headed out toward
the gardens. It was sort of hard to believe that Mohonk was
so close to Oyster Point, where people like Barbone lived,
and to the Oyster Hut, where locals flocked for fried sea-
food and French fries and a salad bar loaded up with Kraft
dressing. Not that the restaurant didn't have its charms, but
I couldn't help but think my parents could learn a thing or
two from Mohonk, where the menu posted by the information desk boasted things like frisée salads and truffles and
Cornish hens.

"We should split up," I said as we headed into the shrub
maze. "If you find the clue, shout out that you got it and
we'll all meet back out here."

So we all headed off down different hedge paths, and I

soon hit a dead end. When I turned back around and went out to where I'd come from, I picked another path to head down and, that quickly, I was totally turned around and lost. But this path led to another two, so I picked one of those and figured I'd run into somebody—and hopefully the clue—eventually.

I was only wandering for a second before I heard Dez calling out, "I got it," and I felt sort of sad that it was already time to leave the maze. I'd often daydreamed about being wealthy enough to vacation at Mohonk and I wanted to get lost in a daydream today, maybe one about Carson, and how it was all going to shake down tonight, or in the next few days, that it really *was* me he wanted. How the whole Winter thing was a misunderstanding.

"Focus," I said to myself, and I methodically started to take notes of turns I was making. It seemed to take forever for me to find my way out, and the others were calling out— "Mary! Hurry up!"—which only made things worse. We were never going to win the whole thing if I couldn't get out of the damn shrub maze. And then there it was, the exit, and there was Dez, holding a piece of paper and saying, "There were like fifteen copies of it so maybe we're the first ones."

"What's the clue?" I reached for it

"What took you so long?" Patrick asked.

"I got turned around," I said to him, then repeated, "What's the clue?"

Phones buzzed and we all read the text. The Yeti said: NEXT TEAM AT FLYING SAUCERS GETS FREE FRIES TO GO ON THE YETI AND ALSO A BONUS 50 POINTS JUST BECAUSE.

Oh well.

"The clue," I said, and Dez said, "'Find Mohonk's clipper

extraordinaire/helmed by a remarkable pair/The name of the ship/is the point not to skip/if you want a shot at a marvelous dare.'" He looked up. "Any ideas?"

"None," Winter said.

"This list is way too clever." Dez handed the clue to me and I read it again.

"Seriously," Patrick said. "I guess this is what happens when the list maker spends a year at Yale? I mean, who would have expected? Though technically, the rhythm of the limerick is off."

We all just looked at him.

"What?" he said. "It is!"

"I sort of thought we'd be playing beer pong and flashing our tits," Dez said, then nodded toward the girls and added, "Or, your tits."

"There's still the second list." Winter absentmindedly adjusted her bra strap. "Our tits aren't out of the woods yet."

"Let's hit the gazebos and think," I said. So we headed off toward a delicate-looking wooden plank bridge over a small valley near the lake, and snapped a picture of the gazebo on the bridge, then headed off to photograph another one up higher on the same path. It was Winter who said, "Hey, guys, this sign says Skytop Road."

"Wasn't there something about a Skytop on the list?" I asked.

"That's why I mentioned it," Winter said. And I wanted to throttle her. But not in front of the others. For a second, I thought about texting her about Carson but that seemed ludicrous even to me with her standing right there.

It's complicated, she'd said.

What the hell did that mean?

"Take your high-tops to the sky top," Patrick recited.

"Fifty points." Then he pointed at his shoes and said, "Once again my outfit saves the day."

"It's true," I said, with a bit too much enthusiasm, but with Patrick I was now all about trying to keep tension at bay. "I am sorry I ever mocked your chosen attire." I bowed down to him, like servant to master, and he smiled.

"The sign says it's a fifteen-minute walk," he said.

"Round trip or one way?" I asked, then read it for myself: "Fifteen minute walk; Pleasant but steep." A line below said, "More challenging walk to Skytop via the Crevice, 100 yards to your right."

"Only one way to find out," Patrick said, and moved toward the path.

"We don't have time," I said.

"I'll go alone," Patrick insisted. "If I hustle, it won't take me fifteen. Then I'll meet you by the docks. And in the meantime you figure out the clue. We don't lose time if we divide and conquer."

"Okay," I said, feeling relief that Patrick was still thinking clearly about the hunt, even if he wasn't thinking clearly about me. "You have your phone to take the picture?"

"Yes, Mary," he said, sort of annoyed-sounding. "I have my phone. But wait. Give me yours."

"Why?"

"The word jumble. It's only on your phone."

"Oh, right!" I said, and handed him my phone and only then thought of the texts to Winter. But Patrick wasn't the sort to poke around somebody else's phone. Was he?

Anyway, it was too late.

He had already taken off up the Skytop Road toward the tower atop the hill.

"I guess we need to go into the hotel," I said, turning to Dez and Winter. "Maybe just ask someone?"

"I hate asking people things," Dez said.

"Well, I think we're probably the only idiots who drove all this way for a dopey one-point clue," Winter said. "So let's just do it. We can't leave without asking because then the whole thing might be a waste of time."

"That's the spirit," I said, annoyed. What was up with *Winter* acting pissed? She knew I liked him, so she shouldn't have gone and liked him, too.

"What?" she said. "Sorry. I just mean, it might be a big waste of time so let's hurry. That's all."

"Fine," I said. "I wasn't saying we shouldn't hurry."

So we went back across the wooden bridge and down what felt like hundreds of steps, then up the long paved path to the resort, which loomed large in front of us like a mountain in its own right.

There was a woman working there and I asked her whether there was a clipper ship connected to the resort or to its history. She thought for a second and said, "Not that I'm aware of." Then right as I was about to say, "Okay, thanks anyway," she said, "But there's a painting in the conservatory of an old ship, if you want to go look."

"Could we?" I felt a seed of excitement that we were on the right path.

"Of course." Then she gave us directions.

So we headed down a long hall and up a staircase and then down another one and through a lobby, then followed signs to the conservatory and found the painting. The placard below said only, THE FLYING CLOUD CLIPPER.

I reached for my phone then remembered, and felt naked for a second. "Google it," I said to Dez, who took out his phone. I watched over his shoulder as he typed in "*Flying Cloud* Clipper" and found it on Wikipedia.

I read highlights aloud: "Set a record for the sail from New York to San Francisco, with a female navigator. Captained by her husband. Known as an extreme clipper because of its speed." I looked up. "So this is the answer. *Flying Cloud.*"

"But what does it mean?" Winter asked, but I could barely look at her.

"Nothing's clicking," Dez said.

I looked at the clue again. "It says the name of the ship is the point not to skip." I looked up. "I think we just need the name and it'll mean something later."

"You're sure?" Dez asked.

"I'm pretty sure," I said. It was the only thing that made sense, so I said, "To the docks!"

There was no sign of Patrick on the path leading down from the Skytop tower so we all sat down on the dock even though the very act of it, sitting, felt wrong. It also felt, well, good. Because the air felt different at Mohonk—liberating, somehow, like a blank slate. While it was possible we'd run into classmates here, it seemed unlikely, and that made me happy.

Dez lay back on the wobbly boards that stretched out into the lake and said, "You guys can just pick me up here later. Cool?"

"I wish I could live here," I said, lying down, too, and letting my bones adjust to the planks beneath me. I tried to imagine I was on a more comfortable lounger, perhaps with a glass of wine—and Carson—next to me.

Because he could still like me.

Right?

He had to!

"You'd get bored living here," Dez said, but he didn't sound convinced. I held up Dez's phone and snapped a photo of him and his clothes, which had a shimmer to them that was so right with the lake glistening right beside it, and the glow of Winter's hair was like something out of a movie about angels, a movie Winter would actually want to play herself in, all soft and striking and lovely. I changed the mood of the scene entirely when I said, "So what's going on with you and Carson that's so complicated?"

"That's my cue," Dez said, but as he went to get up, Patrick appeared on the dock and I knew that the conversation would go no further. Patrick just wasn't the sort of guy who tolerated much in the way of gossip or drama and we all knew it. Dez lay back down and I started tracking a thick orange koi that was swimming in the lake and taking occasional nibbles on a lily pad floating near the dock.

"Mission accomplished," Patrick said, and I asked, "Did you send it to the Yeti?"

"I did," he said wearily as he lay down.

He handed me my phone and said, "Winston Churchill."

The word jumble was still on the screen and I worked it out in my head and yes, he was right. I sent a text to the Yeti that said: WINSTON CHURCHILL and the text came back: GOOD JOB.

While I waited for more, maybe another clue, I snapped another photo of my friends—*Sit by the dock of a bay. Or lake*—to send to the Yeti and suddenly Patrick's suspenders didn't seem so bad and I only wished I could somehow be in the picture, too.

"Google them together and see what happens," Patrick said.

"Huh?" I said.

"Godzilla and Winston Churchill."

"On it," Dez said. "But for the record, I am Binging, not Googling."

"Whatever, man," Patrick said.

Dez studied his phone for a minute and said, "It turns up some movie called *Godzilla Vs. Biollante*. The plot has something about Nazis plotting to kidnap Churchill."

"Fascinating," Patrick said. Then he said, "What about your clue? The maze?"

I said, "We got the name of the ship—the *Flying Cloud*—and that sounds like all we need for now. Right?"

"What do I know?" he said, shrugging while lying down.

"Well, can you read the clue again and tell me if you agree that all we need is the name of the ship?" I held it out to him but his eyes were closed.

"Patrick," I said, waving the piece of paper in front of him.

"What?" he said.

"Read it," I said.

He took it and said, "Yes, I agree, Mary. It sounds like we just need the name of the ship." He handed it back and I caught Winter's eyes and saw something flash there, something like sympathy, or an apology. I wasn't interested in either.

My phone buzzed and it was a text from Carson:

HEARD BARBONE MISSED THE RINGING THE BELL POINTS BY LIKE TWO MINUTES. HE IS GOING DOWN!

"Barbone missed the bell points by like two minutes," I reported to my team.

"How'd you find that out?" Dez asked, and I said, "Carson just texted me," and I felt strangely proud of that.

"Awesome," Dez said, without much energy, and I just let

the update soak in. Then another text came, this one from the Yeti and it said: BIG POINTS ON THE LINE OVER AT ASTROBOWL. STRIKE OUT IN THE NEXT HALF HOUR AND YOU GET TEN POINTS FOR EVERY PIN.

"Aw, crap," I said. There were more texts we'd gotten throughout the time we'd been at Mohonk. Ten points here. Five points there. Most of them not big enough to warrant a second look or a moment's regret.

"Well, we knew the risks," Dez said.

We sat there without talking and I just listened to the wind in the trees and the far-off laughter of actual Mohonk guests, and the sounds of boat motors and birds—wondering whether any of the birds from The Pines had followed us here, whether Patrick was right that there was something menacing about them. I couldn't be sure anymore. We probably sat there for longer than we should have, but I didn't want this moment to end—even with all the weirdness. That extreme blue was gone from the sky. It was softer now, like a blue fleece baby blanket, and the softness of it felt right.

"What if you Google Godzilla, Winston Churchill, and the *Flying Cloud* all together?" Winter asked.

I didn't think the game clues had anything to do with the Mohonk clue but I Googled them all together anyway, careful to put Winston Churchill and *Flying Cloud* in quotes, and then I scanned the results.

• <u>IMDb: TV Listings</u>
www.imdb.com/tvgrid/2011-04-16/0115
Godzilla remake; monkey supervillain; Huggytime Bears; . . . . . The team checks out a rare REO *Flying Cloud* hot

rod from the 1930s; . . . A letter signed by *Winston Churchill*;
Holy Relic; gas-fueled remote-controlled toy Hummer. . . .

• Cacha Style: Here's what I had to fix on my
*cachastyle.blogspot.com/2011/.../here-what-i-had-to-fix-
on-my.htm* . . . —Cached

Jul 5, 2011—THE MONEY IS FLYING AROUND THE ·
reo *flying cloud* . . . . . Last edited by *Godzilla!*; 21-09-2010
at 05:34 PM. . . . . . . Nice body, . . . myself and my friends use
BMWs · Na parkingu było fajne miejsce · *Winston Churchill's*
Daimler . . .

• Flying Model | POPULAR GIFTS BY AGE
www.populargiftsbyage.info/flying-model/—Cached

Flying Cloud 50" Museum Model Sailing Ship Replica
$699.99 . . . . . . *Winston Churchill* used one as his own
transport aircraft. . . . . . The monster spewing flames in
Godzilla, the flying bicycle in E.T., the rampaging dino-
saurs in Jurassic . . .

"Not sure it's turning up anything useful," I said. "It all
seems sort of random. But wait, somebody Google 'REO Flying Cloud hot rod' while I keep looking."

"On it," Dez said. Then a moment later, "It's just an
old car."

"Wait," Patrick said. "On the list. Doesn't it ask for the
Yeti's favorite band? Maybe it's *REO* Speedwagon?"

"Hold on," I said, having scrolled farther down and found
another phrase worth following up on and then Googling
"flying cloud thunderclap eruptor," which turned out to be
an old cannon. I shared this tidbit with the group and then
we fell into silence.

Nothing was clicking.

Patrick said, "It says 'stick your neck out for clues' so that probably means that the Hangman game gives a clue to the Yeti's favorite band. So just send in REO Speedwagon."

"I just don't think it's right," I said. "It doesn't feel neat enough."

"Just send it," Winter said. "It's only a ten point deduction if we're wrong."

"Fine," I said, then sent the text.

SORRY, the Yeti wrote back. BETTER LUCK NEXT TIME.

"Told you," I said to my team. "That's not it."

"We should go," Patrick said, lifting his torso up and resting back on his elbows.

He was right.

It was time to get back to the business of the hunt for real. We'd spent almost an hour at Mohonk—a big risk, considering we were walking away with only 101 points, which brought our total to 994—so the Flying Cloud clue had better pay off.

I checked my phone but there was still no response to our having solved the Winston Churchill jumble, then we all stood up and, from the way we did, bodies all slow and tight, you would have thought we were zombies climbing out of our graves.

"I'm sleepy," Winter said, and I said, "You'll get over it."

"We need some fast points," Patrick said, and he and Dez started brainstorming on the way to the car while I tugged on Winter's arm so that she'd lag behind.

"So?" I said.

"So I like him," she said, and she shrugged a shoulder

I was about to say, "But you know I like him," but instead I said this: "He has a girlfriend."

"I know," she said, "and I feel bad about that, but he doesn't even like her like that anymore."

I said, "Well, he should tell her that!"

"He will," Winter said, and she looked so sure of it, so cocky, that I hated her for a minute.

"I don't believe you," I said, trying on righteous indignation for size. "Jill's our friend."

"I bet if he were breaking up with her for you, you'd feel differently," she said.

My face burned and I walked faster, to outpace her, as if that would prove anything, and everything around me seemed shaky, the way things are when the heat is bouncing off the ground beneath your feet on a hot day. Then I got back into the car, where I sat and fumed and tried to read the list. Winter followed a minute later but we didn't make eye contact in the backseat.

"I think we need to hit the ninety-nine-cent store," Patrick said, oblivious. "The rest of the weird kitchen stuff. Maybe the maple syrup. There must be more."

"Sold!" said Dez, with a worried look in the direction of me and Winter. "Or at least let's head that way until we think of something better."

We didn't think of anything better—though we did argue about the best place to get a 12-pack of Bounty, and whether or not chocolate chip banana bread would bake eventually in a parked car on a day this hot, if we could find all the ingredients and a pan.

Our phones all buzzed simultaneously when we were a few minutes outside town: BE THE FIRST TEAM TO TAKE A BUBBLE BATH AT THE SHALIMAR AND WIN 200 POINTS.

We didn't even have to talk about it.

Patrick said, "On it," then stepped on the gas and Winter said, "We need soap. Bubbles."

"The 7-Eleven," Dez said. "It's on the way."

"We never emptied the shampoo from Eleanor's," I said. "It's in the trunk."

"Just drive!" Dez yelled.

Patrick made a sharp right turn and I screeched, "What are you doing? The Shalimar is that way!" I pointed.

"Mary," he scolded. "Calm down. I know a back way."

So I said a prayer that he wasn't about to screw this up that went like this: *Please, God, let him not screw this up.*

And then, sure enough, the glowing gold lights of the Shalimar—the very catering hall and ballroom where prom had been held—came into sight around the bend in the wooded road and we pulled into the circular driveway out front. It was eerily still, even with the fountain pulsing. There was no one around.

Dez said, "Holy shit. We really did it," and I grabbed the shampoo bottle from the trunk and Patrick and I headed for the fountain. Winter and Dez quickly undressed down to their underwear and hid in the bushes lining the Shalimar's circular drive, and I knew it was mine and Patrick's turn to strip down to our intimates as soon as the fountain looked amply bubbly.

We'd taken a picture first of the non-bubbling fountain and sent it to the Yeti, then we'd sent another one of Patrick with the shampoo bottle. One more pic after we got into the water and we'd be done. I felt giddy that we'd actually succeeded in getting there first and giddier, still, that we might be able to flaunt our success to other teams who were still on their way here.

We needed a new team name.

We were no Also-Rans.

"Is it just me," I said to Patrick, "or is the water getting bluer?"

He studied the plumes of water and then the frothy bath by our knees. "Definitely bluer," he said. "Like a nice shade of toxic."

"What is this stuff, anyway?" I tried to read the label on the bottle in his hands so that I could see the brand name. "People wash their hair with this?"

"Explains a lot, really." He gave the bottle a squeeze.

"Like what?"

"Like why old ladies have blue hair."

The thundering fountain filled the air around us with mist and Patrick dunked the now-empty bottle under the water and then poured it out. "I guess I just don't understand," he said, and I braced myself, knowing he wasn't still talking about blue shampoo or hair. "We share everything. We're closer to each other than we are to anyone else by a long shot, and I mean, why not at least give it a shot?" He shook his head. "So what if it doesn't work out. At least we tried."

"I'm *really sorry*," I said slowly. "But I just don't feel that way about you."

"Is it because of prom?" He seemed to, well, stiffen.

"No." I shook my head.

"Because guys get hard-ons, Mary." His eyes bore into me. "Deal with it."

With that, I kicked off my shoes and walked around to the other side of the fountain, where I'd be hidden by its plumes as I stepped out of my shorts as fast as I could then stepped into the fountain. I slipped off my top just as my underwear got submerged, and lifted it off over my head just as my bra went in and tossed it aside and went underwater, lying back like I really was in a tub. I stayed under as long as I could, fountain jets pulsing against me, eyes closed against the toxic blue. I wanted to stay under longer—maybe look for some secret passage to the lost city of Atlantis—but my lungs burned with longing for air so I burst up to the surface.

Patrick and Dez and Winter had climbed in. Dez used his phone to line up the shot of the three of us, while Patrick took two heaping handfuls of bubbles and propped them on his head to make a big white bubble-fro.

Dez said, "Smile!" like it was two syllables and took the picture.

"All right," he said. "Let's go."

Patrick climbed out—wet, with blobs of bubbles sliding down his bare back to his SpongeBob boxers—and we all followed, grabbing our clothes and heading for the car. I was almost disappointed that no one was chasing us away from the Shalimar because I felt like running.

Very far and very fast.

Away from Patrick and all this awkwardness.

Away from Winter and her secret and my own jealousy about it.

And from high school and Barbone and everything else.

"Two hundred freaking points," Dez said, and he high-fived me and I met eyes with Patrick and he seemed somehow more disgusted with me than ever before.

A few other teams had arrived as we started putting our clothes back on to wet skin. Tom Reilly's car just kept on going; no point in stopping once the points were already claimed. A few teams we didn't know cruised by shouting out curses and insults. Only Carson's team stopped.

"Are you guys going to hit twelve-fifty?" Carson asked, and it was Winter who said, "Of course we are."

"Awesome," Jill said. "Us, too."

Back in the car, Dez was adding up points and said, "We've got eleven ninety-four." Then, "Guys, if we rearrange the hay in the park for sixty points, we're in the next round."

"Really?" I said. The park was just a few minutes away. "Hay bales and we're done?"

"With time to spare," he said, then he nodded and high-fived me again and I didn't care what Patrick thought. He was the one who was going to have to *deal with it*.

WE OYSTER POINTERS HAD MIXED FEELINGS about the "art installation" in the park overlooking the waterfront on Stomp Hill, which was basically a bunch of hay bales that the artist expected us common folk to rearrange for our own amusement. Some, including my father, argued that bales of hay can't be art and dubbed the artist "some earthy crunchy nut job with too much time on her hands." Others claimed the nut job was a visionary. Still others argued that just getting people to talk about what art *was* was sort of the whole point. When I'd decided to actually read what the artist had intended when her statement appeared in *The Oyster Pointer*—"The project is intended as a translation of the geometrical geography that was, and is, still necessary for productive agricultural labors and will depict the overlap between this original morphology of the cultivated land and an idealized and abstract pattern of the Cartesian knowledge"—I couldn't help but side with my dad.

In the last few weeks, the hay bales had—according to *The Oyster Pointer*, at least—been arranged into the shape of a peace sign, some unfortunately square snowmen, a penis, and more.

"What about building a stairway-to-heaven-type thing?" Patrick offered as we stood in front of the hay bales, which were arranged in the shape of a phallus again. So some of our classmates had clearly already been there; probably Barbone.

"Too hard," Winter said.

"That's what she said," Dez said.

If you only knew, I thought, careful to not make eye contact with Patrick.

I *knew* guys got erections.

I was *perfectly prepared* to deal with it. When the right guy and the right erection came along.

"Think easy," Winter said then. "Think outlines. Think the sort of crap a four-year-old draws. Butterflies and flowers."

"But we could get extra points for being clever," I said, remembering for the first time the Special Points. "We haven't even been thinking about special points and how to get some."

"Well, I don't do clever," Winter said, and Dez said, "Give yourself some credit, Winter. You can be clever."

"Name one time when I was clever," Winter said, and I laughed.

Even when you were mad at Winter, it was hard to be mad at Winter. She rested her head back on a bale of hay and said, "Let me know when you special people come up with something."

"Let's look at the list," Patrick said. "Maybe there's something else we could get points for? Like if it's a picture of something on the list or something?"

"See, now that's brilliant!" I said, too enthusiastically, judging by Patrick's look, and I took out my list and sat on a hay bale just in time to see Carson's team pull up and park behind Patrick's car. One by one, they all got out and strolled over to where we were sitting and trying to be clever.

"Are you guys done?" Jill asked with hands on her hips, and Dez said, "Do we seem like the types to make a penis to you?"

Jill laughed. "Not exactly, no!"

I said, "We were just going to start. Why don't you come back in fifteen minutes?"

"Fifteen minutes?" Jill looked at her teammates. "Why don't we just help you guys then we'll do our thing?"

"That's okay. We can handle it," I said, feeling myself quickly tiring of this conversation, though I wasn't sure why. Maybe because Jill was obviously oblivious to everything that was going on in her own boyfriend's head.

"What are you going to make?" she asked.

"We don't actually know yet," Patrick said, and I felt a little bit annoyed that he'd admitted it.

"Well, then, just let us go," Jill said. "We'll be really quick."

"But we just need to do this and then we're into the next round," I said. "So if we want to really have a shot at Barbone, you just need to let us do this. Okay?"

"But," Jill said, "we only need to do this and like one other thing to get to the next round, so maybe we should go first so we'll have time to get the last fifty points." She looked at her watch and it annoyed me that she was wearing a watch—was that some kind of statement?—and she said, "There's time."

"We were here first," I said sharply, and it seemed like all of my friends just froze. I knew how it sounded. What was I? Eight years old?

"We're all on the same side," Jill said, and I said, "Well, I mean, we are. But I'm the one who really wants to stick it to Barbone, you know?"

Not even eight years old! More like five!

But it was true!

"Fine," Jill said. "Be that way. But you still don't know what you're making and we'll be done by the time you figure it out." She started walking toward the hay bales.

"Carson," I said, turning to him, though why I thought he would be the one to help me out I have no idea. "Seriously?"

He shrugged and said, "We'll be quick," then walked past us all and, that quickly, he and Jill and Heather and Mike were rearranging hay bales to take the shape of . . .

"What the hell are they making?" I asked. "And why am I the only one who's annoyed by this?"

"That's a really good question," Patrick said. "Why *are* you so annoyed?"

Maybe it was silly to get so worked up about Barbone taking the Yeti to Georgetown, but it suddenly mattered very much that it was my team who won it. Dez and I, at least, had been tolerating Barbone since kindergarten so I felt he was ours to take down. I didn't say any of that, though—only looked at Winter, who wouldn't make eye contact—and so we just stood there and within the next few minutes, Carson and Jill's team had managed to make an igloo. A *small* igloo, yes. They'd barely used a fraction of the hay bales available, but it was an igloo nonetheless.

"Why didn't we think of that?" Dez said, and Patrick said, "Because we're thinking too hard, trying to be too clever."

"Speak for yourself," Winter said.

Carson's team had already snapped a picture and they were all heading for his car.

"I don't know, Mary," Jill said by way of parting, "I thought we were all in this together."

"Well," I said, "we are and we aren't." I was trying to lighten the mood but it wasn't working. "I mean, it *is* a competition, right?"

Jill shrugged and said, "That's fine. Two can play at that game." She walked off.

"Come on," I said to my team. "We're running out of time."

Patrick, Dez, and Winter followed me to the middle of the field, where the igloo had been built, and then Patrick said, "What was *that* about?" He lifted one of the bales off the igloo.

"I just think it was bad form for them to cut in front of us." I tried a bale but could barely get it to budge.

"But what's the big deal?" Patrick said. "They're our friends."

I said, "Can we just do this and then talk about it? I mean, I'm sorry, okay?"

Patrick sighed and wiped some sweat off his forehead. The day had gotten hotter, or maybe it was just us. "What about Stonehenge?" he said.

"You don't think someone's already done it?" I said. "It's so obvious."

He snapped, "Well if it's so obvious, why didn't you think of it ten minutes ago?"

Then Winter, who was making a last-ditch attempt to find inspiration on the list said, "A goldfish?" She got her phone out for reasons I couldn't even imagine, and set about sending a text.

Dez said, "But for the goldfish item it specifies it has to be alive."

"Well, I tried," Winter said.

"It doesn't really matter what we make," Dez said. "We should just qualify."

My phone buzzed and I went to look at it. The text was from Winter and said: JUST BECAUSE YOU'RE MAD AT ME DON'T TAKE IT OUT ON EVERYBODY ELSE.

I didn't even know what to say, so I wrote: I DON'T KNOW WHAT TO SAY.

"Are you two texting each other?" Patrick asked.

"Of course not," we both said.

I looked at the igloo and thought about Stonehenge and tried to think of other famous structures, then had an idea. "What if we take the top off the igloo and make the whole thing a little bit taller and crooked, like the Leaning Tower of Pisa. We can have one of us pose like we're holding it up."

"It'll never look enough like the Leaning Tower of Pisa," Patrick said. "It'll just look like a silo or something. How about the front wall of a castle? Like with a gate and a turreted sort of tower on each side."

"It doesn't really matter what we make!" Dez shouted this time, but Patrick and I were locked in this, I'm not even sure why.

"I can't picture it," I said.

"I'll just show you," Patrick said. "Trust me, it'll be good. We'll tell the Yeti we've built him a castle."

"Awesome," Dez said. "Let's do it."

"We don't have enough manpower," I said. "Let's just do Stonehenge. We can make it small."

"Fine," Patrick said.

"Let's just get on with it," Winter said.

"Yes, for the love of god," Dez wailed.

The bales were awkward and heavy. We had to work in teams of two, so we decided to do so in one girl–one guy pairs. Patrick was paired with me and when we were far enough away and when Winter and Dez started talking, Patrick said, "Did you *tell* her?"

I lied and said, "No, I didn't *tell* her."

"Well, what was that about then?"

"Nothing," I said. "Girl stuff."

"Give me a break, Mary." Then he was about to say something else but my phone buzzed.

It was from the Yeti and said: APOLOGIES FOR THE DELAY. THE YETI IS RATHER BUSY: 21 13 12 1 21 20.

"Who is it now?" Patrick said with annoyance.

"The Yeti," I said. "Something in code. To build on Godzilla and Winston Churchill."

"Well, we should finish this first," he said. "So we're in for sure."

Hayhenge, as Patrick started calling it, was starting to take shape. And we were lucky to have Dez on our team because he was sort of petite and easily hoisted on Patrick's shoulders to help shift bales into position. We were almost done when Barbone's car rumbled onto the park road.

"Ugh," Dez groaned.

"Are we almost done here, guys?" Winter asked with some dread in her voice, and Patrick said. "Almost."

Barbone approached with a "What the hell is that? Some weird shrine to gayness?"

"It's Stonehenge," Dez said, then he added, "Douche bag." It was said in a whisper, near Winter's ear, but I heard it. And if I heard it, that meant . . .

"What did you say, choirboy?" Fitz asked.

There was a weary edge to Dez's voice when he turned and said, "I said, *douche bag*."

I watched as Fitz started to turn an angry sort of red in the face.

Then, in case it wasn't clear, Dez said, "I called Jake Barbone a douche bag."

"Oh, man," said Fitz, looking at Barbone. "You're not gonna take that shit lying down, are you?"

"Whatever, man." Barbone got this dumb grin on his face and he said, "Me and Daphne here, we go way back. Don't we, Daph?"

"That we do," Dez said, and I just wanted Barbone to go away. Or to die. It wasn't a nice way to feel, hating someone as much as I hated him, but there was no way around it.

Barbone gave Dez a funny look, then he turned to his friends again. "See, I don't even know how you get to be the kind of person that talks like that. 'That we do!' But you know what I do know?"

"What?" asked Fitz. Allison and Chrissie were smiling dumbly into space.

We had one last hay bale to position to make Hayhenge complete, and it required that Dez climb up on a sort of makeshift step stool we'd built out of hay once we'd realized Patrick couldn't hold Dez for that long and still be useful to us.

"I know," Barbone said slowly, "that you don't mess with fags because you get in more trouble than when you mess with regular guys."

"Don't call me a fag, douche bag." Dez was high up on the hay bales now. "And while we're at it, how about you stop calling me Daphne."

It was Fitz who shoved the bale under Dez. It wobbled and he lost his balance and fell back away from us, to the other side of Hayhenge, where he landed on the ground hard with a thud.

The next sound was Dez's scream.

Barbone said, "What the hell, Fitz?" and Fitz held up a hand expecting a high five but was denied.

I rushed to Dez's side.

"Shit," Dez kept saying, "shit shit shit."

"What is it?" I asked. "What's hurt?"

"My wrist," he said. "It's bad." He was cradling it with his other hand.

"Not cool, dude," Barbone said to Fitz. "I *just said* we weren't going to mess with the fag," and they headed off toward more hay bales with the girls trailing behind them like mutes.

"Can you move your fingers?" I asked Dez, because that seemed somehow important, and he could, but he could not move the wrist without screaming.

"What are we going to do?" Winter asked, and I said, "Dez. We need to get you in the car, okay?"

I helped him up and he winced but he could walk, of course, so he got over to the car and into the backseat without too much trouble.

"Shit, shit, shit," he said once we'd all gotten back in. And he fanned a hand over his face to cover tears. The injured wrist lay on his lap and was already starting to purple.

Patrick said, "I think our next stop is going to have to be the hospital."

I was about to argue—we could ice it, wrap it up tight, so that we could get back to The Pines to qualify for the second list—but then Dez moaned, "Holy mother of God."

Almost like a reflex, I turned to the backseat shelf, and saw that Mary was no longer there. "Where's Mary?" I asked, in a panic.

Winter looked around by her head, then by her feet, and said, "The trunk?"

I shook my head. "No. I put her up here."

Winter said, "Yeah, you're right. She was definitely back there before. When we were at Flying Saucers for sure."

"I honestly don't believe this," I said. "Someone took it."

"But who," Patrick said.

"I don't know!" I said. And then I *did* know. "It was Jill," I said. "She said 'two can play at that game' like it was some kind of threat."

Patrick sort of laughed. "Well, you *were* being pretty obnoxious."

"They were the ones who wanted to cut in front of us!" I honestly didn't get why they didn't get it.

"It's just wasn't that big of a deal, Mare," Winter said.

"What about stealing Mary?" I asked. "Is that a big deal?"

"Well it seems pretty obvious," Patrick said, "that she is trying to prove a point. And I'm sure she'll give it back."

"I think the bigger deal is that my wrist is broken!" Dez shouted.

The Yeti's text said: FORTY-FIVE MINUTES TIL CHECK-IN, SCAV HUNTERS! MAKE IT COUNT!

The radio was on and Patrick switched it off but Dez managed, "No, leave it. I like this song and it's a good distraction from all your pathetic bickering."

The song was that hit-you-in-the-gut anthem "Beds Are Burning," by Midnight Oil, one of those random songs that the DJs on WOPR felt the need to play at least five times a day. Even though the song was really old, I knew all the words and had downloaded it and I felt certain that when I heard it in ten or twenty years, it would magically transport me back to a feeling, to a moment. I did not want it to be this moment.

The time has come to say fair's fair.

The car felt eerily quiet even with the music blasting. What was there to say? Why did people like Barbone and Fitz even *exist*?

To pay the rent. To pay our share.

Why did Dez have to go and bait Barbone?

How can we dance when our earth is turning?

What did that even mean?

How do we sleep while our beds are burning?

I felt sick about the way I'd behaved with Jill—an also-ran like me, though she didn't even know it yet—and about Carson and Winter, whispering sweet nothings in front of Dora and Diego—*¡Ayúdame!*—and about the fact that after all that work we'd forgotten to take a picture of Hayhenge.

Without Mary we were down to 1094, and out of the running.

I was screwed.

Not just today, but in life—where people like Barbone got into better colleges and got better jobs and cars and Yetis, and girls like Winter got guys like Carson. Good girls like me, even reluctant ones, went nowhere fast—I was living proof!—and now Dez wasn't the only one crying.

AT THE EMERGENCY ROOM ENTRANCE, I STUDIED
the sky again. It seemed to be slowly draining of blue as the
sun's angle had begun its shift toward evening, and I felt
drained, too. I wiped away tears with two hands, palms full
on cheeks, and turned to Dez. "Ready for your close-up?"

"I can't believe this is happening," he groaned, his
eyes wet.

"You guys go in with Dez," Patrick said. "I'll park."

So we got out and went through the ER doors. At the main
desk, a nurse about my mother's age, and with the same hair
color and style—a short brown bob—looked up and studied
us for a second. I said, "We think my friend's wrist is broken."

She looked over at Dez's wrist, unimpressed, and said,
"Sign here and have a seat."

"Right handed," Dez said, lifting the injured wrist with
his left, and the nurse shot me a look, so I picked up the pen
attached to the sign-in clipboard with a piece of string and
wrote Dez's name. We backed away and shared a look that
said, *What's her problem?*

The waiting room was otherwise empty of emergencies,
though I was pretty sure I could scare up a few if I tried.

The Virgin Mary's been kidnapped!

My heart is breaking!

I'm going away and I'm scared to death!

We sat and waited and I texted Jill to say: DID YOU GUYS TAKE THE MARY STATUE FROM OUR CAR?

She wrote back right away: NOPE.

"Jill says it wasn't her," I said, and Winter looked at me like I was some kind of monster.

"Really?" Winter said. "That's your concern right now?"

"It's worth a hundred points! And it's the closest thing I have to an important family heirloom or whatever."

"Well, you should have thought of that before we took it!" Winter said.

"It's okay," Dez said to Winter, and Winter folded her arms across her chest and looked off toward the TV screwed into the wall.

To me, Dez said, "Let's talk it through to keep my mind off this." He nodded at his wrist.

"I can't remember the last time I can be sure she was there," I said quietly so as not to disturb Winter and her current snit, though what reason she had to be in such a bad mood was beyond me. She probably wasn't thrilled that everything seemed copacetic on Carson's team, which meant still no breakup, but that was hardly my fault.

"Me neither," Dez said. "So it could have been taken at the hay bales—by Barbone—or at the bell or at Party Burg or Flying Saucers."

I said, "Well, that sure narrows it down." We'd crossed paths with at least five teams, if you counted the ones who'd been spotted by the Shalimar while we were taking a dip.

"My money's on Barbone," Dez said.

"But we would've seen them near the car," I said. "Right?"

"I don't know, Mare."

A nurse came out and called Dez's name and he got up and said, "You guys should go. Bring me Barbone's head on a plate."

And before either of us could say anything he was through a set of double doors and gone.

"You're not mad that I like him," Winter said.

"I'm not?" I think I guffawed.

She shook her head. "You're mad that he likes me."

Patrick came into the ER then and I stood up, ready to go, but Winter didn't move and Patrick sat down next to her and put Dez's backpack on the chair beside him with a thud. "Did anybody call his dad?"

"I'm not sure that's the best idea," I said. "I mean, what if his dad calls Mullin or the cops and the whole hunt gets shut down?"

"*Let it go*, Mary," Winter moaned.

I spoke slowly and deliberately, as if each word were its own sentence, when I said, "Dez just said we should go back out there!"

"He did?" Patrick asked, sounding pleasantly surprised, I thought, and Winter and I both nodded.

"Well, we're not just leaving him here," he said.

"We can come *right back* after we get the second list!" I said.

"I'm calling his dad." Patrick got up and walked away, phone in hand.

"I'm sorry he doesn't like you," Winter said then, but I could think of no reply, no words worth saying.

When Patrick came back a few minutes later, he sat down, looked at the time on his phone and said, "So I guess we're done."

I nodded—from my own phone I knew it was 5:25—and faced straight ahead at the TV. Looking up at it I read some headlines on the news channel's crawl, each one more depressing than the last.

3-year-old boy drowns in lake in Cleveland, Ohio, suburb. . . .

Mayor of Pennsylvania town accused of "sexting" teens . . .

Victims of fire remembered in Maine.

I pictured *Girl fails miserably at scavenger hunt during senior week* and *Girl's best friend steals her only romantic prospect* and thought I was going to cry, again, and then I did. Not full-on but I had to wipe my eyes and Patrick said, "Hey," and slid into the seat next to me. "I know you were all fired up about this, but I mean, who even wants to do the hunt with nothing but A-holes for competition?"

"But why should they have all the fun?" I said. "We're better people."

"Yeah, and we know that." Patrick adjusted his suspenders. "We don't need the Yeti to prove it."

"I hate him," I said. "I really hate him. And I hate the way it makes me feel." The tears were streaming steadily now, and I was powerless to stop them. I wasn't even sure it was about Barbone anymore, but I couldn't explain everything else, not to Patrick.

He took a breath. "Let's see what they say before we pack it in for the night, okay?"

I wiped my eyes. "But we're down one hundred because of the missing Mary and if we stay here and wait, there's no time. And we never took a picture of Hayhenge, so that's another sixty we thought we had that we don't."

Patrick produced the Dixie cups from his bag and said, "I

need a pair of scissors." He got up and asked at the nurse's station and the nurse who looked like my mom obliged.

I nodded approval as he started cutting triangles from the cups, then I looked through the list again for the icosahedron's point value—65, which seemed super low considering how complicated it was—then read looking for things that could add up to another 91 to get us to 1250. I stopped when I got to origami sheep.

10 points per.

Ten sheep.

I checked the ER clock again.

I had no idea if it could even be done.

"How many copies of the list do you have there?" I asked Patrick.

"Four," he said, after a quick count. "Why?"

I searched on my phone for "origami sheep."

I took the staple out of one copy of the list and started folding.

"What are you doing?" Winter asked.

"Origami sheep, ten points each so we'll need ten." I folded again.

Patrick said, "Now that's the Mary I know and love," and the word *love* clung to the air like a spiderweb—fragile, delicate, and complicated.

"I need tape," Patrick said, when he appeared to be done cutting, so he got up again.

Winter got up and said, "And I need to find a restroom."

"So what's with you two?" Patrick asked when he came back, and I said, "Oh, it's nothing. It'll pass."

"You're a terrible liar, Mary."

"Sometimes," I said.

"Hey," he said. "What about that clue? In code?"

"Oh, crap," I said then found it on my phone.

I read the numbers out to Patrick and he wrote them down and then wrote out the letters of the alphabet with numbers next to them. "It's probably a pretty simple code," he said, and he set aside his half-made icosahedrons and got to work. After a few minutes of scribbling he said, "Umlaut."

"Huh?" I said.

"That's the clue. Umlaut."

I must have looked entirely confused.

"You know, two dots over a letter."

"I know what an umlaut is," I said. And I typed into Google all three of the hangman clues—Godzilla, Winston Churchill, and umlaut—and it turned up gold.

• Blue Öyster Cult—ArticleWorld

www.articleworld.org/index.php/Blue_Öyster_Cult—
Cached

May 20, 2011—Two other well-known songs are "*Godzilla*" (1977) from Spectres, . . . by *Winston Churchill's* description of Italy during World War II. . . . The addition of the *umlaut* was suggested either by Allen Lanier or Richard Meltzer. . . .

• Blue Öyster Cult—Wikipedia, the free encyclopedia
*en.wikipedia.org/wiki/Blue_Öyster_Cult—*Cached

Their next album, Spectres (1977), had the FM radio hit "*Godzilla*," but its sales were . . . . from a phrase used by *Winston Churchill* in describing Italy during World War II. . . . The addition of the *umlaut* was suggested by Allen Lanier, . . .

• Blue Öyster Cult Artistfacts

*www.artistfacts.com/detail.php?id=196—*Cached

. . . "Soft White Underbelly," after a *Winston Churchill* quote describing Italy in World . . . The band's name is properly rendered with an *umlaut* over the letter *o*. . . . They did the most incredible version of *Godzilla* (no drum break). . . .

"Blue Öyster Cult," I said, heart already racing. "It's the Yeti's favorite band!"

"Send it in!" Patrick said. "Wait. What's Godzilla have to do with the Blue Öyster Cult band? Or Winston Churchill, for that matter? Or an umlaut?"

"Don't know, don't care," I said, and sent this to the Yeti: YOUR FAVORITE BAND IS BLUE OYSTER CULT.

Then I studied my search results again and said, "There's an umlaut on the *o*" and texted: (WITH AN UMLAUT ON THE O)

I unfolded one fold of my sheep-in-progress to confirm it was 100 points, minus ten for that one wrong guess. "Ninety points!" I squealed and the Yeti wrote back and said, THE YETI IS BURNING, HE'S BURNING, HE'S BURNING FOR YOU!

Patrick held up a hand to me and said, "Dude!"

We high-fived but he grabbed my hand as we did and held on a little bit too long. We had enough points to qualify. We had 1269, if you counted my two origami sheep. And Patrick was putting the last piece of tape onto his icosahedron.

Dez's father came in a few minutes later, winded, and ran a hand over his fine hair. "What *happened*?"

We exchanged looks and Patrick said, "You better let Dez tell you."

Mr. Mahady walked off to speak to the nurse then, and she took him through the double doors. I watched their heads bob and then disappear down the hall, and I started to gather our things. But not a minute later, he came right back out and he said, "He wants to see you all."

Patrick led the way and we found Dez sitting on a bed with his wrist propped up on a pillow. "What are you still *doing* here?" he pleaded.

Patrick set Dez's backpack on the chair beside the bed. "What did they say?"

Dez said, "They have to do an X-ray, probably an MRI."

"Crap," Patrick said.

"Yeah." Dez nodded. "Now get the hell out of here and bring me Barbone's head on a plate. And, you know, the Yeti."

"Don't you mean Fitz's head?" Winter asked, and I had been thinking it, too.

"I'd take his, sure. But mostly Barbone's."

"At least he sort of tried to protect you," I said, surprising myself. Was I *defending* Jake Barbone?

"By *calling me a fag*?" Dez punctuated the question with a laugh of disbelief.

"I didn't mean—" I said, but now I didn't know what I meant.

"You know," Dez said, "sometimes I wonder whether any of you are any better than guys like Barbone and Fitz."

"What are you *talking* about?" I said, feeling suddenly very tired.

"You're not going to get it," Dez said, shaking his head. "And I'm too tired and doped up to deal with you all right now. You're not going to make it back by six unless you leave like this second."

"Dez," I said. "We can't leave things like this."

"Yes, we can," he said. "Because you're quitting this thing over my dead body."

"We can't just do it without you," Winter said sadly. "It's not right."

"It is, *too*, right," Dez said. "If you can't win it with me, win it *for* me."

A wave of excitement started to swell somewhere deep down in my gut because I could see it in Winter's and Patrick's eyes that they seemed to be warming to the idea. And there seemed to be a sort of skip in time in which we were all frozen and then, just like that, we tore off running out of the room, then down the hall, then out of the hospital and around the corner to the parking lot, where Patrick fumbled with his car keys and I said, "Hurry, hurry, hurry."

We were maybe a five-minute drive from school and Patrick drove faster than he had all day and the radio was still on and the car was filled with fuzzy guitar licks and drunken sounding notes and a guy singing, *Things weren't going my way . . . but I feel luckier today.*

The moment felt suddenly imbued with meaning and some kind of universal import. Maybe it was some kind of message from the fates, an encouraging omen to say that things—the hunt, our rattled friendships, college, *life*—were going to work out fine after all. Because even if I couldn't win Carson away from Jill and Winter, I could still win the hunt, the Yeti.

I turned and looked at all my local landmarks whirring by—just Laundromats and parks and paint stores and Party Burgs—and wondered about what lie ahead for us that night. What other teams had made it? What would the second list be like? Would there be anything illegal or sexy or scary on it? Did I want there to be? Was there really *any way* that people like me could beat people like Barbone? And who on earth had taken Mary?

It was Patrick who got a text right then and he looked up at me, confused. "What?" I said, thinking something awful must have happened—something *else* awful—and then he put his phone down and turned into The Pines and said, "Carson just asked if he could join our team."

WE WERE BACK WITH EXACTLY TWO MINUTES to spare, so we got out of the car and waited. Nobody really knew how eliminations would work—how long they would take—but I hoped for a few minutes, at least, to investigate the fate of Mary.

"So?" Carson appeared, all jolty like a puppy. "Can I be on your team?"

"I guess!" Patrick said. "But why?"

I held my breath, feeling a little excited and a little scared, too, the way I felt during the handful of times in my life when it felt like something was actually *happening*.

"Wait," Carson said. "Where's Dez?"

I said, "Barbone said something obnoxious and Dez called him a douche bag and Fitz pushed the hay bales Dez was standing on and he's in the emergency room with a broken wrist. Or *possibly* broken, we don't know yet."

"And you left him there?" Jill asked, having appeared, wide-eyed, next to Carson.

"He said to!" I protested.

"His dad is there," Patrick added, and that seemed to satisfy Jill.

"What total assholes," Carson said, looking over at Barbone's team, who were whooping it up across the lot. Then he looked back. "But you're going to do the second list?"

"Dez wants us to," I said.

"Okay, now you *have* to let me be on your team." Carson was nodding fast.

"But"—Patrick shot a confused look at Jill, who was already walking away—"I'm confused."

"Jill and I broke up," Carson said.

"What?" Patrick said. *"Why?"*

I stood perfectly still and tried not to look at Winter.

Carson said, "It's been coming for a while."

"Wow," Patrick said. "Sorry. And, I mean"—he looked at me then and I just raised my eyebrows dumbly—"of course you can come with us."

"Is that cool, Shooter?" Carson asked me then, and the nickname felt all wrong and it was like he knew it—it sounded hollow—and I regretted ever having allowed him to use it in the first place. I said, "I don't know. I mean, we might be going back to get Dez and there's not a ton of room in the car."

Winter looked at me like I was not only a monster, but a two-headed one.

I wasn't proud, but that's how I felt.

I did not want Carson on our team.

I didn't think I should have to watch whatever was going to happen with him and Winter play out right under my nose.

"We can make room," Patrick said.

"Fine, then," I said. Because what else was I supposed to do? I could join Jill's team, I guessed. Or quit all together, but I didn't want to abandon everything I'd already worked so hard for, and didn't want to abandon Dez.

"Winter?" Carson said then, and she uncrossed her arms and said, "Sure, I guess."

"I'm going to try to find the Mary statue," I said, not caring for a minute what anyone thought, then I went straight over to Barbone, and stood hands on hips. "All right, Barbone. Give me the Mary statue."

Barbone's eyes found mine and he smiled. "I have shucked a few virgins in my day, Mary, but yours was not one of them."

"I don't believe you," I said.

"Believe whatever you want," he said, and he pulled a statue of Mary—not Eleanor's—out of his car. "But why would I need yours if I have this one? Hey, how's Daphne?"

"He's in the hospital." My hands tightened into fists. Seeing Barbone here, so smug, was making it all so much worse. I wanted to scratch his eyes out. So when he said, "Wasn't me," with wide eyes and hands spread, palms out, I said, "I'm going to try to get you disqualified."

"Knock yourself out," he said, then he said, "Tell Dez he's got to toughen up before college. And you, my dear, need to *get over it*."

Then he walked off and shouted, "GO HOYAS!" and I was standing there stunned and ashamed and thinking, *How do people get to be like this, like human cinder blocks? And how are people like me supposed to deal with them?*

My phone buzzed: DID YOU QUALFY?

It was Grace. Grace who was probably drunk.

YES. ARE YOU DRUNK? I wrote back.

BUZZED my phone buzzed back.

I looked over to the five or six cars all parked facing one another other, around a keg, at the opposite end of The Pines and spotted her leaning on a car that I knew had been part of Round 1. There were maybe only six or seven cars that seemed to be lined up with Barbone's and ours for judging.

I walked over and said, "Are that many people out of the running?"

"Apparently, some people got bored and just want to drink," Grace said. "And the others just didn't get enough points."

"Someone took Eleanor's Mary on the Half Shell," I blurted.

"What?" Her eyes were a little bit unfocused. "Why?"

"It was on the list," I said. "Shuck a Mary on the Half Shell. So I took it, but somebody stole it from us."

"You are so screwed," she said slowly.

"You think I don't know that?" I shook my head. If anyone understood how deep the shit was that I was in, it was Grace. "So I take it you haven't seen it."

She shook *her* head then nodded toward the LeSabre. "Isn't that your team with that judge guy right now?"

I looked over and saw Lucas with a clipboard, peering into the trunk of the car so I bolted over. He nodded hey and smiled and I said, "Hey. I have a question." Actually, I had two and I had to make a quick decision as to which to ask first. "That team over there—"

I pointed at Barbone, and my friends gathered closer. "One of their guys pushed one of our teammates off the hay bales and he's in the hospital. Shouldn't they be disqualified or something?"

"Let me talk to Leticia," Lucas said, then he walked off.

"Mary," Patrick said seriously. "You sure you want to do this?"

"I'm sure," I said.

In a moment Lucas was back, with Leticia by his side. "Who did the pushing?" she asked.

"Dave Fitzgerald," I admitted reluctantly.

Leticia shook her head. "Hey, Fitz!" she shouted out, and we all turned and saw Fitz look over. "You're out," she said. "DQ'd."

"What the hell?" Fitz said, and Leticia walked toward him, saying, "Crap like that just doesn't cut it. Not this year. Not with me in charge," and I loved her more than ever.

Barbone looked over to the keg and said, "Yo, Smitty. You're up!"

And so Joseph Smith, aka Smitty, took Fitz's place, leaving Barbone's team certainly no better off, but no worse either.

"Thanks," I said, turning back to Lucas. It wasn't the same as getting the whole team disqualified but it would have to do.

"No problem," Lucas said, then added, "Hey, I go to George Washington."

I cocked my head and said, "That's where *I'm* going."

He laughed and said, "That's sort of why I mentioned it. Your sister told me."

He went back to our list and I felt dumb—of course he'd go for perky Grace—but went about showing him our loot, and then he looked up and said, "You're good for Round two."

"Awesome." I smiled.

"Here you go." He handed me a few copies of the second list. "You can look but you can't start your cars until the whistle. Good luck. And hey, nice work on the umlaut."

"Thanks," I said, letting the realization that it was Lucas on the other side of those texts sink in. "One more question for you," I said.

"What's up?" he said.

"Have you seen a lot of Mary on the Half Shells so far?"

He considered a second. "None, but you're only my third team. Why?"

"Because I had my great-aunt Eleanor's Mary on the Half Shell but somebody took it from our car and I *really* need to find out who and make sure I get it back by the end of the night."

"Oh, crap," Lucas said.

"What?"

"That was my idea." His eyes apologized. "I put that on the list."

"Well, how were you supposed to know?" I said.

"I feel bad, though," he said with a wince. "I promise I'll be on the lookout, okay?"

"That'd be great," I said. "The one Barbone has isn't it, just FYI. Unless he shows you a second one."

"Got it," he said, then he took off.

"Who was that?" Winter asked. "I don't remember him."

"Lucas Wells," I said. "I remember him. He goes to George Washington."

"He's cute," she said, and she elbowed me playfully but I wasn't up for it. Did she really think I'd shift my affections away from Carson so easily?

Carson came closer and said, "Is that the list?" so I handed him one, then gave one to Patrick, too.

I started reading, looking for anything to do with the Flying Cloud clue. But when I saw that there were things on the list that only one team would be awarded points for, I flipped to the last page and started to read backward, so I'd maybe see something we could do before anybody else even got to the list's last page.

Patrick went to get into his car and Carson said, "I thought we'd take mine?"

"Why?" Patrick asked. "I don't mind driving."

But everybody knew why.

"We'll have more room for more crap and there's more room for Dez," Carson said, diplomatically dodging the issue of Lexus vs. LeSabre. "Jill took everything and is finishing out with Mike and Heather. So we can leave all your stuff here and just combine all the stuff when we get back."

It was a perfectly logical reason. Even Patrick couldn't argue with that and appear sane, though I could tell he felt a little one-upped.

"Okay," he said, closing the driver's side door and locking the car after we'd all grabbed our bags. "I guess."

When he called shotgun on the way over to Carson's car, I had to push down some annoyance that I'd have to be in the backseat beside Winter. But then I found it, the sort of thing I'd been looking for on the list. "Guys, be ready to go the second they blow the whistle."

"Okay, why?" Carson said, but the whistle came then and, with the grunt of the engine, we were on our way out of the parking lot.

"Where am I going?" Carson asked, and I threw a quick salute to the Yeti and pictured bringing him into Dez's hospital room just a few hours from now, victorious, and said, "Take the right toward town."

Winter said, "What's going on? Where are we going?" and I said, "We're going for a gondola ride!"

Right then, Jill's car went by and her window was rolled down—Mike was driving and Heather was in the backseat, hair blowing wildly, but they'd failed to pick up a new fourth—and Jill looked right at Winter, whose window was also open, and shouted, "I know what you did!"

Just before she was out of sight she added, "Real classy."

A little bit shocked and looking entirely mortified, Winter turned to me and I gave her a sort of *what-did-you-expect* look then turned away, though I was just as confused as she appeared. I studied the backs of the boys' heads in the front seat and felt my stomach flip and not in a good way because I very much wanted to be very far away from both of these boys—and from Winter, too—and probably *should've* changed teams. Looking away, back toward the The Pines, I saw my sister talking to Fitz.

In the front seat, Patrick looked up from his own list and said, "And bam! Skinny-dipping!" He laughed and looked back at Winter. "We'll have to tell Dez I got to see you two naked after all."

I texted my sister and said, STAY AWAY FROM FITZ!

She wrote back EYE EYE CAP'N just as Patrick turned in his seat to face Winter. "So what did you do that's so classy?"

"Yeah," I said. "What's *that* about?"

I watched the tendons in Carson's neck tighten when Winter said, "God only knows."

It sounded entirely like a lie.

"NIGHTTIME IS THE RIGHT TIME"

- An unopened box of Kleenex (in case we get emotional at judging)—20
- A coffee mug (ceramic)—10
- A red-and-black screwdriver—40
- A pillow (in case we get sleepy at judging)—20
- A fan (in case we get overheated at judging)—40
- A remote control (yes, another one)—10 plus 10 bonus points if remote control goes with aforementioned fan
- A bib—10
- An alarm clock—20
- An acorn—50
- A gel pen—25
- A sock—1
- A can of tuna—3
- A toothbrush—3
- Picture frame—5
- A red crayon—10
- An abacus—40
- Teapot—30
- Tape dispenser—30
- Bobby pin—30
- Change purse—25
- Bundt pan—30
- Last year's yearbook—30
- Ticket stub from any *Twilight* Saga movie—75
- A wedding invitation—80
- A bathing cap—75
- Go fly a kite (and take a picture)—80

- A picture of at least one team member with someone with a moustache—100
- Any comic book featuring Superman and dated before 2000—50
- A business card from Susan Witherton—50
- A piggy bank that is not actually a piggy—45
- A sub from Blimpie—20
- Completed crossword from yesterday's *Oyster Point Advance*—75
- A rain poncho—15
- A Ping-Pong paddle—20
- An inflatable SpongeBob SquarePants inner tube—100
- An E-ZPass—50
- An eye examination chart—100
- Shave Bob's balls—80
- A pair of dice—20
- A photograph of a local ghost—80
- A hard-boiled egg, decorated for Easter—75
- A trepanation Barbie—80
- A scone—25
- Is the next Hemingway or Franzen on your team? Write us the opening paragraph of a novel about Oyster Point High—100 to best author only
- A cooked number 8 spaghetti noodle, al dente—20
- Put the union rat to work—100
- You have been an eyewitness to some really bad teaching these past four years. We want the police sketch of the culprit—125
- Any likeness of Pooh (but not with Tigger)—40
- The largest thing you can take from Mr. Gatti's property—100 to largest
- Save water, drink beer, go Wunderbar!—80

- A condom—15
- A bouquet of flowers—50
- Tag the town red—100
- A beer cozy—30
- Gumhenge—45
- Set up camp somewhere uncampy—75
- A martini (shaken not stirred)—80
- A stain-free, completely clean family-size bucket from Kentucky Fried Chicken—35
- Be the first team to say "salut!" to the gondolier. You know the one.—100
- A stain-free, completely clean copy of *Penthouse* magazine (so we can read the articles!)—80
- Give us your best Lloyd Dobler—100 to the best only
- Convince a stranger to deliver one of your Scavenger Hunt items to us before 9 P.M.—80
- A 3 x 5 index card—5
- A bar of soap from a hotel—10
- A squirty toy—35
- A silhouette profile of one of your team members—40
- A plant that falls under the category of *succulent*—50
- Go skinny-dipping. We don't care where so long as you are naked and wet. *All* of you. Send multiple pics if required—200

10

THE RADIO WAS LOUD AND AWESOME SOUNDING—
some new Spoon song—and everything felt new. The meters
and knobs on the dash were shinier, the seats more comfortable, the air cooler and cleaner. Even Patrick seemed to be
distracted by our new ride, rubbing the leather by his knees,
fussing with the handle above his door where his hand
finally settled with a cling so that his arm hung in front of
the window. And with Carson behind the wheel, driving
with race car–driver swagger—totally confident, totally in
control—Patrick—up there in the passenger seat with rainbow suspenders and knobby knees—looked more than ever
like a big kid.

How was it possible so much had happened in one
afternoon?

Rolling down my window and letting the wind whip my
face, I slipped my hair out of my pigtails, put it in a ponytail
instead, then assessed my work as best I could in the car's
side-view mirror. I looked good—different—and that felt
right, because I *felt* different. Betrayed. Stunned. But something else, too. Maybe excited in an entirely new way. Because
things, for better or worse, were actually happening tonight.

Life was happening.

Was this what things were going to feel like all the time next year? When I was out in the world on my own?

The nature of the game, the hunt, had changed completely now that we were onto the second list, and I could feel it—some kind of shift in my brain and in my body, like my blood had started pumping in the opposite direction. We were no longer going for a minimum; there was no set goal. We needed any and all points, and fast, if we were going to win and take home the Yeti. There could be no wasted time, no opportunity for points lost. It was time to get real, to get serious.

With Carson no longer mine for the taking, the Yeti was all I had; the only way to turn the night around was to win and win big so that I could hold it over Barbone forever.

A text from the Yeti said: SIX TEAMS REMAIN. ALL HAD SOMEWHERE BETWEEN 1269 (LESABRE) AND 1540 (BARBONE!) SO YOU ARE STARTING ROUND 2 NECK AND NECK. GOOD LUCK!

"How did Barbone end up qualifying with more points than we did?" I asked, feeling the fire being stoked in my belly.

"Don't worry about it, Mary," Patrick said, sounding a little exasperated.

"I'm telling you he has Mary on the Half Shell," I said. "And he's just hiding it out of spite." I felt sick whenever I thought about Eleanor's statue, out there in the world without me.

"But he said he didn't have it?" Patrick asked.

"Yes, and I don't believe him," I said.

"But if he had it," Winter said, "don't you think he'd want to rub it in your face?"

"Maybe," I conceded. "All I know is if we don't get it back, I'm dead."

"Why?" Carson asked. "What's the big deal?"

"It's like a family heirloom," I said. "My aunt bought it in Italy at the end of World War Two."

"Oh," he said, "I bet it'll turn up." Then he turned up the radio during the song's guitar solo and rolled down his window and let out a scream. He rolled the window back up again and smiled, pounding out the drumbeat on the steering wheel.

"Sorry, guys," he said. "And I'm sorry if it seems really mean but I feel *so freaking awesome* right now." He seemed to be looking for Winter in his rearview but she was looking firmly out her window.

Patrick sort of laughed and said, "Okay," like Carson was a mental patient.

Carson turned the music down a little bit and said, "I just mean, this thing with Jill has been weighing on me for weeks now and I was so dreading the actual breaking up but now that it's out there, I feel like I could just do a cartwheel."

"Well, if it were on the list," Patrick said, "I'd say go for it, but otherwise, maybe not."

"I don't even know how to *do* a cartwheel," Carson said, "but you get the idea. I feel . . . I don't know . . . *free.*"

I looked at Winter to see if I could read her face, but she was still staring out that window. But if Carson felt so great being free, that didn't seem great for Winter if she'd been thinking the two of them would be together now. Was that what was going to happen next? Were Carson and Winter going to become a couple? And how was I going to stand it?

The list, I said to myself.

Focus.

136

So I read through the whole thing and didn't find what I was hoping to find. "There's nothing about the Flying Cloud," I said. I didn't understand.

"There has to be," Patrick said, flipping pages.

"So you guys went to Mohonk, too?" Carson asked.

"Yeah," Patrick said.

I was sort of disappointed that ours wasn't the only team who'd done it but hopeful that Carson had information to share. "Do you know what it means?" I asked. "The clue?"

Carson said, "We assumed there were more clues coming."

"Us, too," Patrick said.

"Oh, and I have this." Carson reached into his back shorts pocket at the next light and took out a folded postcard. "Since I could bring one item with me." I saw that it had a picture of the New Orleans Mardi Gras parade on it. "It's seventy-five points."

"Maybe there will be a text clue?" Winter said while I added up our new total, 1344.

"It has to be," I said. "Unless it was a wild-goose chase. Or maybe the clue is connected to something here somewhere, but we're not seeing it?"

"I'm pretty sure we'd see it," Patrick said. "It's smarter than we thought it would be, sure, but there is no real genius at work here."

I wasn't so sure and thought that maybe there was a trick or some kind of hidden clue we just couldn't see yet. "What about the fact that the Flying Cloud is an old car. Should we be looking for antique car dealerships or something?"

"Possible," Patrick said.

"I'll Google," I said, but the results were underwhelming. There seemed to be some classic car auction in a different Oyster Point, this one in Virginia, but none in ours.

"Who's Bob?" Patrick asked. "And how would anyone shave his balls?"

"No idea," Winter said. "And gross."

"Why are balls gross?" Patrick asked, with some edge, but no one answered and I just felt mortified and looked out my window. We were in front of a gas station, a few blocks away from Rizzo's.

"Dude," Carson said finally. "Come on." He smiled over at Patrick. "They're pretty gross."

Patrick just looked out the window and shook his head.

My phone buzzed and it was Dez: DID U MAKE IT?

I wrote back, YES. AND WE GOT FITZ DQ'D.

AWSE! Dez wrote.

I sent, HOW ARE YOU?

BORED, he said. WTNG 4 MRI.

He was clearly texting with one hand.

Then he asked: SKINNY-DIPPING?

I took a minute to think of my reply and opted for: AFRAID SO.

Dez wrote back: PATRICK MUST BE !!!!! Then: BAR-BONE DQ'D?

NO, I wrote back. SORRY. Then I wrote: BUT THERE IS BIG NEWS. CARSON AND JILL SPLITSVILLE. HE'S WITH US NOW.

Dez only wrote: !

And I wrote: HE LIKES WINTER. SHOOT ME.

Then: ALSO JILL SEEMS PISSED ABOUT SOME-THING. SAID TO WINTER 'I KNOW WHAT YOU DID.' WHAT DID SHE DO?

NO IDEA, Dez wrote and somehow it *looked* like a lie, even though I knew it wasn't possible for type to look one way or another.

Carson said, "Crap," and pulled the car over to the curb and turned off the music with a quick slap of a button on the dash.

We'd arrived at Rizzo's, where a long red-and-gold awning stretched from the front door to the curb. Tom Reilly's team had already gotten there and Tom himself was on the roof—presumably having climbed the fire escape on the side of the building—where a creepy-looking scarecrow-type gondolier stood in a long and slender boat. It looked more like the kind of guy who'd escort you across the River Styx than one who'd take you on a leisurely tour of Venetian canals, but points were points. Tom had climbed into the boat and was posing for his teammate's cell-phone camera.

"How did they get here so fast?" I said, infuriated. They'd beaten us to the bell at Fort Wayne, too, and were possibly shaping up to be our main competition.

"No idea," Carson said.

"Well, that was a bust," Patrick said. "So what do we do next?"

"Mr. Gatti lives pretty close to here," Carson said as he looked at a copy of the list. "Just past the train tracks."

Mr. Gatti was the theater director at school. Also a science teacher, but only freshman courses so none of us had had him as an actual teacher in years. There was crossover, naturally, between the band kids and the theater kids and Carson was both, having just that year played the lead in *Joseph and the Amazing Technicolor Dreamcoat*.

"But what could we possibly steal?" I asked.

"I don't know," Carson said. "But we should go look, at least. He's got all sorts of crazy lawn ornaments and stuff."

"Okay, drive," I said, and we were off again and I watched Tom and the gondolier fade into the distance. "How did they get there so fast?" I asked again, and Patrick said only, "Let it go, Mary."

"I've always wanted to go to Venice," Winter said. "But not if the gondoliers look like that."

Carson laughed and said, "Don't worry." He smiled at her in the rearview mirror. "They don't."

"All right," I said. "We need to be multitasking even if we're going to Gatti's. Who wants to write the opening paragraph of a novel about school?"

"You should be the one to do that," Winter said, and I said, "Okay," because I felt like I'd been doing it in my head all night anyway: *They were the best of times. They were the worst of times.*

"Excellent," Carson said, and there was a part of me that resented how entirely normal and content he sounded. Had he even *noticed* that I liked him? Did the fact that Winter and I were best friends make him think twice at all?

I said, "'Put the union rat to work.' What does that mean?"

"No idea," Patrick said.

"Who's Susan Witherton?" I asked.

"She's that real estate agent whose face is plastered all over town," Carson said. "She has an office near Stop & Shop, I think?"

"Awesome," I said. "But what time do places like that close?"

"Yeah, it's probably too late," Carson said. "Sometimes they leave little business cards in dispensers outside, though, I think. For when they're not there and people walk by?"

"Doesn't sound promising," Winter said.

"What about a condom?" I said, without realizing how awkward the question would sound coming from me, someone who'd never laid eyes on an actual condom outside of a sex ed class I'd taken years ago.

"I have one," Carson said, and at the next red light, he pulled out his wallet, slipped out a condom, and held it up and out toward the backseat.

I just stared at the shiny square, sort of stunned.

"What do you want *me* to do with it?" I said, and Carson laughed and tossed it into the backseat. Winter squirmed away and the little square just sat there on the seat between us like a dead bug, neither of us willing to touch it. Still, I added 15 points to our total. For 1359.

"You ladies have issues," Patrick said, shaking his head.

As if he wasn't a virgin, too!

But what on earth was Carson doing with a condom? *In his wallet?* Had he and Jill done it? Had they done it in the week since the rumor had started? Or was the condom intended for something—*someone*—else? Like, for Winter? Tonight?

The very thought of it—of Winter and Carson, together, kissing or anything more, made me feel sick. And *so humiliated*, too. All that time we'd spent together working on prom, he and I. All the inside jokes and "Shooters," none of it meant anything and now my brain was stuck on a loop, unable to move past the question of: How could I have been so horribly wrong about Carson and Patrick and *everything*?

We drove in silence for a moment and Patrick said, "So what's the deal? I thought you and Jill were solid."

I clenched my fists and waited.

After a pause, Carson said, "It's been coming for a long time."

"Yeah, you said that," Patrick said skeptically. "You could've fooled me."

"It's hard to explain," Carson said, and his eyes met Winter's for a quick, nervous instant in the rearview. "It just didn't seem like we were going to stay together once we went away, so what's the point of being together now?"

"I guess," Patrick said. "Or maybe you could argue that you should be together now since it's your only chance, and why not."

I felt certain Patrick wasn't talking about Carson and Jill anymore.

"I don't know," Carson said. "I guess my heart just wasn't in it. And I mean, this is our last summer here and our last summer before college. It doesn't feel right to waste it with someone you're not crazy about."

Carson looked at Winter again then, in the rearview mirror, and Winter looked out the window. She sure did like looking out that window.

"She sure seems crazy about you," Patrick said to Carson, as if that were enough—as if one person's feelings could be big enough to count for two.

Had anyone ever written a book or a good magazine article about how to be friends with a guy who wanted to be more than friends? Because that's what I needed. And he needed an article, too, one that told him to stop making me feel guilty. It wasn't like I wanted to hurt his feelings!

The Marriott was coming up fast on the right side of the road so I shouted, "Soap from a hotel!"

Carson jerked us into the parking lot and cut a diagonal line across it then stopped near the hotel entrance and put the car in park.

"I'll go," I said.

Wasting time deciding stuff like that was just that, wasting time. Plus, the car, while luxurious, had started to feel claustrophobic, too small to contain everything that was going on. Weirdness between Patrick and me. Between Winter and me. And, unless I was imagining it, between Winter and Carson.

"This may sound strange," I said, when I got to the front desk.

"But you'd like a bar of soap?" the woman said.

After a split second's surprise, I said, "Yes. Yes, I would." Then felt the need to add, "It's all in good fun. Nothing crazy or illegal or anything."

"Sure," the woman said. "I gotcha."

She called housekeeping and then returned to whatever it was she was doing and I just waited. The lobby was empty except for two men, sitting and talking loudly in a lounge, where a grand piano sat eerily quietly. A woman behind the small bar was reading a romance novel, and I had a hard time imagining a more boring place to tend bar. I wanted to run up to her and ask her how she'd ended up here, and how I might avoid such a boring fate myself, and then I secretly hoped she was writing the Great American Novel and just tending bar here to pay the bills, or putting herself through school in astrophysics. Or something. Anything! Because what if this *was* the best night of my pathetic life? What if things didn't get better after high school but worse?

My phone buzzed and I figured it was the Yeti, but it was only Dez. It said: HOW ARE YOU HOLDING UP?

I sat and wrote: BARELY.

Dez said: TELL HIM HOW YOU FEEL? SO YOU'LL KNOW FOR SURE?

Not even two hours ago, I was sure Carson and I were heading toward some romantic confrontation. What if I *was* somehow misinterpreting everything? What if telling him how I felt could change the course of events?

I was contemplating how to reply when Carson appeared

by my side, and for a half a second I hoped he'd come in to tell me there'd been some big misunderstanding, that he'd only been talking to Winter about me, that she'd misinterpreted things.

"What's up?" he said.

"They're bringing it," I said,

"Awesome," he said. "I've got to run to the loo."

He went toward signs for restrooms and I realized how different it was to be around him now. Now that he was available. It really was now or never, do or die, and I felt certain there was a passage in that romance novel the bartender chick was reading about a moment just like this one, when the timid heroine decides to take her romantic fate into her own hands.

But he liked Winter.

This was no romance novel.

I told Dez: I DON'T SEE THE POINT.

A woman wearing a red Marriot uniform appeared in the lobby and handed a bar of soap to the woman at the desk, who nodded to me, so I walked over and got it and said, "Thank you so much."

Dez said: GOING FOR MRI!

I waited for Carson, thinking *I'm going to do it, No, I can't*, over and over on a loop and then he was back and the moment passed and we walked in silence back to the car, which he had left idling in a handicapped spot out front.

Real classy, I thought, for reasons I couldn't explain.

And it's a bathroom, for the record. Not a loo.

"We're idiots," Patrick said as we got back into the car. "Carson, your parents probably have a drawer full of hotel soaps at home and we're probably hitting your house for skinny-dipping."

144

"I wouldn't say a *drawer* full," Carson said.

"They're practically *never* on American soil," Patrick said, and I knew it was true but something about Patrick's saying it, and so flippantly like that, felt weird. Possibly because Carson's parents had just missed the entire production of *Joseph*.

"Well, it only took a few minutes to get it firsthand," Winter said lightly.

"Sure," Carson said. "And they might not even have any."

"Carson" Patrick said, obviously not picking up the vibe I was picking up, or was he? Was he trying to be hurtful to Carson? Pointing out his parents' jet-setting ways? "Are your parents, or are they not, currently spending two weeks in the South of France?"

"All right, already," Carson said. "So they travel a lot. And yes, they happen to be away, so we can skinny-dip in my pool. And we can boil and decorate an egg there, and cook a piece of spaghetti. What else?"

"We need to stage Gumhenge," I said, adding ten points for the soap to our total, now 1369. "But we need to buy gum first. And do surgery on Barbie."

"We don't have a Barbie yet," Winter noted.

"So we'll need to get one," I said. "Is there booze? Like for a martini or Piña Colada?"

"Probably," Carson said, and I said, "Awesome."

Carson said, "There must be more, too. Keep looking." He nodded at the list in Patrick's hands.

"Hotel soap," Patrick said, shaking his head and smiling. "I'm telling you."

We pulled out of the parking lot and Carson said, "So. Gatti's house?"

"Yes," I said.

Carson nodded at the list in Patrick's hand. "Anything else on the way?"

He drove out toward the train station and I thought about the list—all those objects and tasks floating around in my mind's eye. It was enough to drive a person crazy if you let it. All the points, all the strategizing. And the way your brain was drawn to some things, but not others. Like I had no interest in a French spatula or fettling knife, whatever they were. I'd written off some of the pranks and stunts, too—like shaving Bob's balls, since we had no idea who Bob was; and "Save water, drink beer, go Wunderbar," since we had no idea what that meant either—but realized that was a dangerous way of thinking. You had to be open to everything, hold the whole list—*both* lists—in your head at once and look for opportunities everywhere.

As we passed under the train station, where graffiti clung to cement, I said, "What about 'tag the town red?'"

Patrick snorted. "We're not really graffiti types."

I said, "Says who?"

"Mary," Patrick said sternly.

"What," I said. "I'm just saying that just because we have never *to date* spray painted a name on a public structure of some kind doesn't mean we're not *capable* of doing it."

Even as I said it, though, I wasn't convinced, and that fact made me sad. Maybe we *were* too good to win the hunt. Maybe to win you had to take the sort of risks we weren't capable of taking? But what were we—what was I—so afraid of?

A text from the Yeti read: FIELD REPORTS PUT CARSON WILLIS AT THE MARRIOT AND BARBONE IN MATADOR PARK.

"Wait," I said. "Someone saw us. How'd we miss them?"

"I guess we just did," Winter said, but I took the time to look behind us to see if anyone was following us. Like maybe one of the other teams or the judges? There was something about being seen and reported on that made it all the more exciting. It was really happening. This was it. Not Round 1, but Round 2. The one we needed to win in order to, well, *win*.

"I'm not capable," Patrick said, "of spray painting a public structure. And anyway, why is it tag the town red and not paint the town red. I mean, are you even sure that's what it means?"

"I did it once," Carson said, "but it was different. I was just adding my own graffiti to more graffiti. In Dublin. Near Windmill Lane Studios. Where U2 first recorded their stuff. The whole alley is covered."

Out of habit, my brain crammed an entire fantasy—about a trip to Ireland with Carson, about woolly sweaters and countryside drives and cows and hills and pubs—into a mere second.

"So the odds of you getting caught or expelled from school were pretty slim, then?" Patrick said, sort of obnoxiously and for my benefit.

"Yeah, but I could've been arrested maybe?" Carson shrugged. "I don't know. But I could be convinced is what I'm saying."

"Me, too," Winter said. "But it would depend on what I was writing."

"You're all unbelievable," Patrick said. "Graffiti? Really?"

I said, "We could write 'Dez Rules' or something."

"Yeah," Patrick said. "Because no one would figure out it was us. And that wouldn't get Dez in trouble."

"Okay, so we could write the Also-Rans or something. Jeez"—I tried to sound light—"not my best idea, but still."

"How many points is it?" Carson asked.

"Not nearly enough," Patrick said as I consulted the list again.

"One hundred," I said.

"That's a lot," Carson said.

"Yes," Patrick said, "but when you factor in the time it takes to buy the paint and to do it and the risk of getting caught and arrested, it's not that many. Not when you can"— he consulted his own list—"get the same amount for skinny-dipping."

"Here we go with the skinny-dipping again," I said, throwing my hands in the air.

"Didn't you guys already do that at the Shalimar?" Carson asked.

"Pretty much," I said.

"But not officially," Patrick said.

"Anyway," I said, to sum up my thoughts on our overall strategy moving forward, "you have to remember we need the *most points* to win; we're not after a minimum anymore. So anything worth as many points as tagging the town red has to be considered."

My phone buzzed. It wasn't Dez, but Grace: HEARD ABOUT DEZ. IS HE OKAY?

I wrote back: GOING FOR MRI.

Then Grace wrote: ANY SIGN OF MARY?

I couldn't bring myself to answer.

Mr. Gatti's house was a small, beige, shingled cottage a few blocks from the train station, with a big front yard full of flamingos and gnomes and birdhouses and pinwheels. Carson stopped the car right out front.

"What looks big?" I asked.

"I don't like the idea of this at all," Patrick said, and though I wasn't going to admit it, I felt the same way. Then again, we could return anything we took, and they were only lawn ornaments. What was the big deal?

"The flamingo is big," I said, pushing away fear. "And that birdhouse is big, too, if you bring the whole pole."

"Sounds messy," Carson said, then my eyes fell upon something very large by the side of the house.

"Over there!" I pointed. "Trash can."

"We can't take the man's trash can," Patrick said.

"Why not?" I asked. "We'll bring it back."

"I'll go," Carson said, and he got out of the car and said, "Come on, Pat. Live a little," and Patrick seemed about to say something obnoxious—he had this look in his eye when he looked at Carson—but then much to my surprise, he got out of the car and headed across Gatti's lawn.

I turned to Winter and said, "So what did you do that's so classy?"

"You're not going to like it," she said.

"I'm a big girl," I said, watching Carson and Patrick cross the yard. "I can handle it."

"Okay, then . . ." she began, and it was all clear in that instant.

She didn't need to form the words.

The dancing at prom, his hand on her hip, the "real classy," his question about cheating. . . .

"You hooked up with him." I was shaking my head. "That's it, isn't it?"

"How did you know?" Winter looked suddenly more suited to her name, white like snow. "But wait, no," she said. "I mean, it was a kiss. I wouldn't really say hooked up."

"When?" I asked. *"Where?"*

"Prom," she said, and I shook my head and said, "I'm going to have to second Jill's 'real classy' on this one."

I had never talked to Winter like this. Ever. Had never disapproved of anything she had done, really. And it all felt wrong.

Winter liked Carson.

Carson liked Winter.

They'd already kissed.

I should have been happy for her but I wasn't.

"But wait," she said. "How did you know?"

"I'm not an idiot," I said, flatly. I felt like someone was manually wringing out my stomach.

Carson had the trash can, and Patrick had the lid, and they were already putting it in the back of the car and I felt like I had a millisecond in which to make things better, to show Winter some kind of best friend support, but I couldn't find a good word or good thought for her. She had kissed the guy I wanted and everything about that sucked.

Winter had been right. The night *had* turned into a bad teen movie, one that *I* didn't even want to play myself in.

"Success," Carson said when he got back into the driver's seat.

"I can't believe I just did that," Patrick said.

I started a little list on the back of our master copy, called "Potential Points" and wrote, "Trash can. 100?"

Everyone's phones buzzed: HEADS UP. BE PREPARED TO SEND ONE REPRESENTATIVE TO RAINEY PARK TO CHILL OUT AND CHUG A RED BULL AND PERHAPS DISCOVER SOME HUNT SECRETS AT 9 P.M.

"Okay," Carson said, turning down the music. "We need to get serious. What on the list are we going for and what are we just going to skip entirely? What can we reasonably accomplish before getting to Rainey Park by nine?"

I bristled at the fact that Carson seemed to be taking over, leading my team. He wasn't even supposed to be here, and the fact of Dez's being stuck in the hospital and not here with us hit me anew. I texted him and said: ANY CHANCE WE CAN SPRING YOU OUT IF MRI RESULTS ARE GOOD?

Patrick said, "Skinny-dipping is a definite."

"Oh, lord," I said.

"Yes," Carson said. "But we won't have time before nine."

"I still think we should go to my house," Winter said.

"What's there?" Carson asked, not having been privy to our Round 1 brainstorms and the treasures of the Watson household, and Winter said only, "Trust me. Just drive."

I was starting to feel like Dez did, that we were the lamest team ever, especially now that we'd lost him, and for a moment I felt like I was going to cry again. It was too bad there weren't points for meltdowns, maybe 50 per.

Dez wrote, NOT LIKELY WITH RENTS HERE.

A new loop: He'd already kissed her. And she'd kissed him.

THEY HOOKED UP AT PROM, I told Dez, who wrote back BAD FORM. Then followed it with: BUCK UP!

"SOMEBODY COME WITH ME," WINTER SAID,
tentatively, to the car once we were parked outside her
house, a faded gray ranch built into a hill dotted with
shrubs.

"You'll be quieter alone," I said, not ready to support her
in any endeavor. Not yet.

"Yes, but faster with help," Winter shot back.

Patrick turned and said, "Aren't you guys each others'
alibis? Like you're supposed to be at the movies together?"

Winter nodded.

Patrick faced front again and said, "So you both have to
go. In case you get caught. You can say it was sold out or
whatever."

Winter and I just looked at each other. I knew there was
no way around it; I had to go. Winter, who knew it, too, said,
"You can look for a toy made in the U.S. in Poppy's room
while I get everything else."

"Okay," I said. "Sure."

A text from the Yeti said, ANYTHING MADE OF RED
GLASS: 25 POINTS.

"We'll strategize while you're gone," Carson said, then

shook his head. "Is it possible we've only gotten ten actual points and a hundred *possible* points so far this round?"

"I'm afraid it is," Patrick said matter-of-factly, while looking at the list. "But Winter's house is actually a pretty big score." He turned to us and said, "Look for a red crayon. And red glass."

"Okay," Winter said, "but we're sneaking in, so there's a lot of stuff I won't be able to get to."

"Just do your best," Carson said.

We headed for Winter's bedroom window, which we'd jimmied open more than once over the years, and we climbed in like we had all those other times, stepping up onto a few cinder blocks stacked in the garden bed, and helping each other as best we could.

Winter's vanity mirror was stuffed with photos of us all taken at different events this past year. Like homecoming last fall. And the Halloween party at Mike Owen's house, when Winter and I had gone as Daisy and Violet Hilton—a pair of Siamese twins who'd been famous in the 1950s. I stood there for a moment, losing myself in the pictures—so many of them—and tried to imagine what next year's pictures would be, what our new friends would look like.

"I don't want you to be mad at me," Winter said, pulling the Siamese twin photo out of the mirror's edge.

We'd been so fired up about that costume but now, tonight, it was hard to imagine us wanting to be joined at the hip.

"You can't control who's mad at you," I said, and Winter said, "Thanks, Dr. Phil." Then she sat on the bed and said, "I just don't understand why you're so upset. I mean, I screwed up, but it's not like he was *your* boyfriend. I wasn't doing anything to hurt *you*."

Winter put the picture back, pulled her *Breaking Dawn*

ticket stub from the mirror, and said, "Patrick's a really good guy."

I groaned. "Of course he is. What does he have to do with anything?"

"It's so obvious, Mare," Winter said, pulling Pictionary out from under her bed and putting a box of cards in a shopping bag she'd found; we'd pick an easy word to draw for the Yeti later, for a possible 35 points. "The way he looks at you."

"What's your point?" I asked. "That I should like Patrick and not Carson? It doesn't work like that!"

Winter just looked at me, and I said, "You should just admit it was a shitty thing to do to me."

"I didn't do anything to you!" she shouted, and I shushed her.

"We're best friends!" I protested, more quietly.

"I can't control who I like!"

"Neither can I!"

I pictured our argument as if it were a line drawing for Pictionary, a precarious tower of exclamation points that had peaked and then toppled.

A moment later, I said, "When did we start keeping secrets from each other?"

"I don't know," Winter said. "I guess I knew none of this would go over well and I didn't want to deal."

"I still wish you'd told me."

She opened her closet and fished a Barbie out of a shoebox. "Well, I told you tonight and see how that's going."

"I just don't want us to have secrets. I mean, it's only going to get harder to stay close next year. We're all leaving."

"No, *you're* all leaving." Winter was enrolled in Fairleigh Dickinson, a short drive from home, where she'd be still living for at least one year until she could maybe save money to dorm. At least that's how she explained it, though I secretly knew she wasn't ready to leave Poppy.

"It's just D.C.," I said, though it was true I'd been acting like I was going away to Timbuktu. "You can come visit. It's drivable. It's trainable. It's flyable. It's only like five hours by car!"

"You know it's not the same," Winter said, then she added, "D.C. is a whole new world." She sighed, pulling stuff out of the bottom of the closet. "I thought you'd go to NYU and that we'd be able to visit each other all the time."

She seemed on the brink of tears and I whined and said, "Winter, come on!"

"What!" Winter said. "I'm allowed to be sad."

"I'm sad, too!" I went to sit on the bed.

Winter looked over. "But you're disgusted with me right now, so it'll pass."

"Disgusted is a strong word." I took the photo from her and put it back in her mirror.

"Well, I'm excited for you, I really am," Winter said. "I mean about D.C. and everything. You're going to Africa!"

"Well, let's not get ahead of ourselves."

The closest I had ever been to Africa thus far had been at the so-called savannahs of Disney's Animal Kingdom in Florida, where I remember feeling frustrated that we didn't see more animals, closer animals. But at George Washington I'd have the opportunity to study abroad during junior year. There were programs in Japan and the Netherlands and pretty much anywhere you could think of, including Africa.

"What if I'm totally wrong about all this?" I said. "I mean, *international affairs*? I've never even been to Canada."

Winter shook her head. "I was there on the class trip to the UN. I saw you eating it all up, like we were visiting a candy factory and not the most ho-hum place in the world."

"The UN is not ho-hum," I said, all serious.

"See!"

The memory of that day came back to me full force. It had been during Carson's first month of having moved to town and my crush was already developing. I was sure we were checking each other out—circling, mostly. Staring and getting caught. But I hadn't known at the time, when we'd flirted over bagged lunches in a room set aside for class groups, that he would soon start dating Ashley Evans, and then Bradee Moore, and then a few others before Jill—with what felt like mere milliseconds in between—and now here we were, almost graduating, and he was moving on to Winter. All of that suddenly made it seem like there might be something wrong with him, something lacking.

"I'm scared," I said. "I mean, what if this idea of mine is totally random?"

Winter asked, "What am I looking for again?"

"Ouija board," I said.

"Right," Winter said, and dug in again. "But, Mary, seriously. I am going to Fairleigh Dickinson to study *marine biology*. Could anything be more random than wanting to train seals for a living?"

"At least people know what that *is*! You can say, I want to work at Sea World and people will get it. What do I say when my degree is in International Affairs? That I want to be a diplomat?"

"Everybody already thinks of you as a diplomat anyway."

"But why?"

"I don't know, but that prom song fiasco, and then that time when the whole school had detention and you were the one who offered to replace the balloon or whatever. In front of the whole school."

I wanted to take the compliment—saw it as one—but said, "I don't know anymore."

Winter said, "Well, I've certainly gotten myself into a bit of a diplomatic dilemma, haven't I? And I mean, what if *I'm* wrong about Carson? What if he's wrong? And we messed everything up for nothing?"

"Well, you'll find out soon enough," I said. And there was a part of me that *wanted* her to have messed up, wanted the whole thing with Carson to go down in flames, except that she was still my best friend. I wanted her to be happy, to fall in love and swim with dolphins and have her every dream come true. Even if it meant being with Carson.

In theory, anyway.

"We better get moving." She stood with the contents of the shopping bag—the Barbie, the Ouija board, and more— in hand. "I'll go get a Ziploc and a few other things and meet you in Poppy's room."

In the hall, the sounds of women squawking at each other drifted toward us from the other side of the house, and I knew it was some *Real Housewives*, since that was Winter's mom's favorite show.

Housewives.

Such a weird word. And something I never wanted to be.

Because you couldn't be a housewife and also be an ambassador.

"Shoot," Winter whispered. "If *Housewives* is on, where's Poppy?"

She cracked the door to her sister's room open and peeked in, then whispered, "Napping. But if she's taking a nap this late she must be exhausted. You'll be fine."

"You sure?" I asked, and she shrugged, then I shrugged, too.

It had to be done, so I sprang into action.

Poppy's room smelled sweet, like lavender and lollipops. Her breathing was a rhythmic exhale followed by a silent inhale, and it was backed up by the quiet static of a white noise machine perched on a small bookcase. I sat in front of the case—which held as many toys as books—and started my search among a herd of My Little Ponies. But it was pretty dark in Poppy's room, so I had to take each toy over to the Tinker Bell night-light, in order to look for the manufacturing stamp.

Twilight Sparkle. *Made in China.*

Pinkie Pie. *Made in China.*

I thought I would like to see the Great Wall someday, like Great-Aunt Eleanor had. But on the other hand, I wanted to stay in Poppy's room forever—playing games about ponies and fairies and princesses—and never have to grow up.

Winter came into the room and said, "My mother didn't even blink," and then proceeded to disappear again and then come back with Ziploc full of water. She scooped the fish out of Poppy's bowl with a small plastic bathtub she found among the toys and pressed the thing shut. "You ready?"

"They're all made in China," I whispered, and had a thought about how I was no better than those housewives, squawking at my best friend over a guy.

Winter made a beeline for the toy chest across the room and picked up a few and said, "Check these." Sure enough, the old-fashioned letter blocks had been made in the USA. "Should we take the whole set?" I asked.

"Nah," said Winter. "Let's take a *U*, an *S*, and an *A* for some special points."

"And you said you don't do clever," I said, and right then I saw Poppy's Lite-Brite.

"Winter," I whispered and pointed. "Put your name in lights?"

Winter grabbed the Lite-Brite, then snatched a children's book at random.

"Any toy ambulances?" I asked softly.

She shook her head.

"Pooh?" I asked.

"She only has love for Tigger."

I stifled a laugh as she pointed over at Poppy and her plush animal pillow, bearing the face of Tigger.

It was all too much. We were suddenly on a roll.

"Winter," I whispered. "The pillow."

"It's a Pillow Pet," she whispered back.

"Whatever," I whispered. "It's Tigger."

"We already have Tigger."

"But it's Tigger *and* a pillow. Special points?"

She shook her head and smiled like I must be crazy, but she put the shopping bag down and went down the hall and came back with a regular pillow. "On my count," she said, handing the pillow to me, then she went over and lifted Poppy's head. I pulled out the Tigger Pillow Pet and swapped in the other pillow, and Poppy moaned a bit. We froze and waited and then her breathing resumed its rhythm.

Winter gave me a thumbs-up and we backed away, then went back to Winter's room and out of the house, carefully carrying our stash.

"Guys," Carson said, when we got back to the car and he pointed over toward the clearing in the woods across the street from Winter's. "Fireflies."

It was, all of sudden, dusk; the air abruptly cooler —even

damp. You could see the fireflies dotting the field next to the woods, like teeny tiny flickering lanterns.

"We need a jar," Carson said.

Winter said, "I grabbed this," and pulled a tall glass jar full of spaghetti out of the shopping bag she'd brought from the house. "In case there's no spaghetti at Carson's." She set about emptying the spaghetti into the seat-back pocket, much to Carson's obvious disapproval.

"Don't they need airholes?" I asked. "The fireflies."

"Actually, they don't," Winter said.

"Really?" Patrick asked.

"Airholes just dry them out faster," Winter said. "Look it up if it you don't believe me."

"You guys walk," Carson said. "I'll pull the car closer."

The edge of the woods was practically aglow from the number of bugs out there, but I was useless at catching them for some reason, too jittery. Somehow Patrick had already caught three and Winter four and I had caught none. So I sat down on the grass and added up the points from Winter's, an impressive 388 when you counted all the extras she'd thrown in without my even knowing: a red crayon [10], a bib [10], a coffee mug [10], dice [20], an alarm clock [20], a gel pen [25], a toothbrush [3], and last year's yearbook [30]. With the Ouija board [45], ticket stub [75], children's book [20], American-made toy [35], pillow [20], and goldfish [65], that brought our total to 1757.

Plus we had supplies for the points involving Barbie, spaghetti, Pictionary, and putting our name in lights. *And* the potential for some Special Points.

Setting my list aside and waiting, just minding the jar, I thought about the last time Patrick and I had done this, in Eleanor's backyard. It had been during the wind down of a July Fourth BBQ during which Eleanor had insisted on manning the grill and had performed a miracle worthy of the good Lord Jesus: transforming burgers into stones.

"Your family's awesome," Patrick had said as he and I chased fireflies to put inside a paper lantern where a small bulb had burned out. It was a science experiment at best—how many fireflies would it take for the lamp to glow—but the bugs wouldn't stay inside it, seemed determined to be free and get their glow on.

"They're okay," I'd said, because Eleanor had just bored everyone with one of her rants about Sue Fink from the garden club and how she had no idea how to run a meeting.

"I mean that I like being with them," he said, and then he had added, "With you."

There'd been a funny look in his eye right then, a look I couldn't recognize on him, and I'd said, only, "Come on. There are ice-cream sandwiches."

Patrick now sat beside me on the grass, shook his head, then caught another bug and slipped it into the jar. He said, "I'm not sure how I feel about this."

I smiled. "Don't tell me we're going to have a big talk about animal rights or some nonsense."

He shrugged and watched as Carson joined Winter by the trees' edge. "You ever see that *Sesame Street* episode about fireflies?"

"Can't say that I have."

He had his eye on another firefly and hands at the ready, reservations or not. "Telly and Baby Bear catch a bunch of fireflies, but then they look really sad and stop flying around, and they don't glow. So the lady from the Laundromat makes Telly and Baby Bear pretend to be fireflies and imagine how it would feel to suddenly be stuck in a jar."

"Deep," I said.

"Just sayin'."

I said, "We're not going to win unless we take every opportunity to get points."

He shrugged. "I don't really care if we win."

"You don't want to beat Barbone? After what happened to Dez."

I left off the, *after what Barbone did to me*? It was hardly fair to expect Patrick to defend my honor now, if that's what it even was.

"No," he said. "I mean, it'd be great to do it for Dez and all. But in the grand scheme of things I don't know if it's really going to matter that much. It's not going to change things here. Beating Barbone isn't going to make Dez's life any easier."

"But it might make him happier," I said. "Tonight."

"I know. And that would be great. But I care only to a point." He played with a blade of grass. "And I mean, you're still not going to Georgetown."

I was about to say something, like "ouch" or "damn" but didn't.

It was true.

Patrick said, "It's Carson, isn't it?" and I felt my breath leave my body too fast.

Patrick wasn't looking at me, was studying the flies already in the jar. "You like him."

"Patrick," I said sadly.

Because it wasn't about Carson.

"Please," Patrick said. "Just don't, okay?"

I had no idea what was going on. "Don't what?"

Patrick looked off toward Carson and Winter, who were doing some kind of silly impersonation of fireflies, flapping their wings and buzzing. Patrick said, "Don't go for Carson. Please. Not now. Not ever."

"He likes Winter," I blurted. "They kissed at prom."

A funny look crossed Patrick's face and he said, slowly, "That guy is unbelievable."

Winter and Carson were laughing and I said, "Why does he like her and not me?" They were having way too much fun. "I swear," I said, "I never get anything I want."

Patrick just shook his head and huffed, then he stood and said, "Oh, grow up, Mary. And stop thinking so much about what everybody else has and look in a mirror."

"Let's go, guys," he shouted to the others, and he picked up the jar and walked off.

I checked off "Jar of fireflies" on the master list, and counted up our catch—11 bugs at 3 points each, for 1790—before getting up to follow. But I didn't head for the car right away. I just stood there on the grass for a minute and watched the bugs that we hadn't caught. They were starting to fade back into the trees, into the darkening woods, and the light of day was all but gone. I felt sort of sad that I couldn't remember the last time, before tonight, that I'd paid such close attention to the sky. It felt like that must be some kind of sign that I'd lost my innocence and grown up without even realizing it. But as I watched Patrick heading for the car—Patrick who'd proclaimed his love for me—and Carson, right next to him, the love of my life who wasn't—I wondered whether Patrick had been right.

I hadn't really grown up yet.

Not really.

Maybe not at all.

FOR A WHILE THEN, THE NIGHT JUST SEEMED TO whip by and we were too busy, too distracted, for me to be mad or tense or heartbroken or anything. I think I was quietly processing what Patrick had said, but also still feeling stung, and focusing on the hunt made it easy to push away some ugly truths. Why *was* I so jealous of Barbone? And of Winter? And of everyone?

We were driving all over and talking nonstop about the list and rapidly accumulating points. The Yeti was sending texts like crazy, adding items like two-dollar bills and any set of instructions to put together something from IKEA and a collector's spoon from the Statue of Liberty. We weren't sure we'd be able to get any of those things, but it added to a sense of frantic.

There was still nothing about the Flying Cloud.

And no clues about the whereabouts of Eleanor's Mary either.

Dez had had his MRI but that was all we knew.

It was all going too fast for my liking—this cramming in of activity before the meet-up at Rainey Park at nine—and every time I checked the clock, I wanted to somehow rewind the hands of time. I felt that way about high school all of a sudden, too. Like I should have paid better attention. Should have learned more or done more or done less and learned less. As we drove around Oyster Point, I saw the ghosts of my childhood and adolescence everywhere. Up Hylan Boulevard to the right was Lisa Englehart's house, where I'd fallen off the pool ladder when I was maybe eight and cut my knee so bad I still had the scar. A few more blocks down from Lisa's was Danny and Ray Bolan's house, where there'd been some pretty crazy band parties my sophomore year, before the Bolan twins had graduated; Winter and I both had our first beers there together.

And our second and third ones.

Right there on the other side of Hylan was Alphabetland Preschool, where I had gone for dance classes for years, before my interest in the flute and band took over. And there was the roller rink, Skate Odyssey, where I'd had my tenth birthday and also where Patrick and Carson and Heather and Mike and Jill and Winter and Dez and I had gone for a laugh a bunch of times, roller-skating around like idiots to weird songs you only ever heard in roller rinks, one called "Come Dancing" with an organ bit that I liked and that seemed just right for roller-skating and another called "Whip It!"

It was relentless, the flood of memories, with new ones still being made even as the old ones trotted by as if on floats in a parade.

So that was what I would remember?

We went to the Stop & Shop and got the maple syrup in the maple leaf–shaped bottle [75], the SpongeBob inflatable inner tube [100], a rain poncho [15], a beer cozy [30], a kite [potential for 80], a bouquet of flowers [50], a scone [25], a bathing cap [75], the Kleenex [20], the 12-pack of paper towels [10], a squirty toy [35] and enough gum to set up a Gumhenge model when we went to Carson's house for another potential 45.

That was 435 actual points, which I thought was pretty good considering they didn't have any red velvet cupcakes or succulent plants, and we left out a bunch of stuff that we knew we could get at Carson's or Patrick's for free.

With 2225 points to our name, we went to the office of Susan Witherton, its windows full of laminated pictures of houses, and found a little dish full of business cards [50]. Carson called her cell and the fact that she was an Oyster Point High alum who'd done the hunt when she was a senior probably helped when he tried to convince her to personally deliver her own business card to the judges on our behalf. Surely, that would win us some Special Points on top of the 80 we'd get just for having a stranger turn up with one scav hunt item.

Along the way, I set about writing the opening paragraph of a novel about Oyster Point High on my phone in an e-mail to the Yeti. It was worth a lot of points (150, if you won) and it also helped me to hide the fact that I was feeling so conflicted about everything and everyone.

The family Gilhooley had long lived in Oyster Point.

Delete. Delete. Delete.

If you really want to hear about it, the first thing you'll probably want to know is where I was born, and what my lousy childhood was like.

Delete. Delete. Delete.

Jake Barbone awoke one morning to discover that he had been transformed into an insect.

So this was writer's block.

Because I thought I had an awful lot to say about Oyster

Point High but when I considered that someone else might *read* it—and that that someone might be Lucas Wells—that certainly limited things. I could just make up any old bs, really, but it seemed like an opportunity to say something of worth, though I didn't know what. In light of Patrick's scolding, grievances that had seemed really important even an hour ago suddenly seemed small, unworthy.

Carson liked the same radio station as Patrick, the station that played old alternative hits, and I recognized the song playing now and the lyrics of the chorus seemed just right though it was hard to say why:

I close my eyes and I see . . . blood and roses.

I closed my eyes, then.

What did I see?

I saw an image of two army nurses, standing by the bed of a male mannequin, smiling and pretending to take his vital stats. It was a photo I'd found at Eleanor's house, while sorting through crap with my parents, and I'd eventually concluded that it was the strangest photo I'd ever seen. There was an official Army Photography Office credit on the back, but I couldn't imagine why such a photo would have ever been staged or taken. I had seen some old *M*A*S*H* reruns, courtesy of Patrick. I knew people sometimes felt the need for humor in war. But there was something about it that gave me the creeps.

What would Eleanor, who'd lived through an actual war, think of tonight's foolishness? Would she have stolen Mr. Gatti's trash can and Poppy's Pillow Pet? And where-oh-where was Mary on the Half Shell?

After a quick stop back by the hay bales—where we considered re-creating Hayhenge in order to photograph it but then opted instead just to briefly fly our bat kite [80]—we made a quick stop to take a picture of ourselves at a bus stop after a text from the Yeti told us to [30], then decided that before going to Patrick's house—our next agreed-upon destination—a stop at Burger King was in order, especially because the crown [30, which was ten more than the Blimpie sub would be] could easily be procured.

Or so we thought.

When we pulled into the parking lot, noting the crazy long line at the drive-through, Winter said. "Don't you need to be a kid to get a crown?"

"What do they care?" Carson said, and so we went inside and took turns ordering; then Carson said, "I got this," and paid while we argued about whether to stay or go.

"I don't like people eating in my car," Carson said, and I said, "You're joking, right?"

"Not so much," he said, stealing a French fry off my tray.

"We're in a race," I said. There was also the fact that spending time in Burger King on a night like this seemed especially lame.

Winter said, "We'll eat really fast, Mary. Let it go."

"So what's the plan?" Patrick said, unwrapping his Whopper and taking off half in one large bite as we grabbed a table. "Who's going to go to the meeting at Rainey Park?"

Carson put another French fry in his mouth and chewed, then took a sip of soda, and it all had the effect of seeming like a delay tactic. When he swallowed and wiped his mouth, he said, "I nominate Mary."

I was wolfing down some kind of crispy chicken sandwich when I got a text from Dez that said, DOC COMING WITH MRI RESULTS SOON.

"Why her?" Patrick asked, as if I wasn't sitting right there.

"I'm sitting right here," I said.

"It was Mary's idea to sign up in the first place," Carson said. "I seriously doubt you'd be here if it weren't for Mary."

"Yes," Patrick said, seeming annoyed. "I suppose you're right."

"I don't care," I lied. "You go if you want to so badly."

I capped it with a single-shoulder shrug. I didn't want Patrick to feel like he was bestowing some gift upon me out of the kindness of his heart.

"No," Patrick said. "It's okay."

"I vote for Patrick," Winter said, and I looked at her, stunned. "What," she said. "I think he'd do a really good job of finding out what everyone's up to and stuff. Everyone likes him."

"Well, thanks," Patrick said, smiling big. "One vote for me!"

I said to Winter, "You just told me everyone thinks of me as an ambassador."

"True," she said. "But Patrick's more . . . well . . . popular."

I was about to argue, but didn't. It was true.

"Why don't either of *you* want to go?" Patrick asked, and Carson and Winter both shrugged.

It was obvious to me Patrick was baiting them, even though that seemed unlike him. He had even less reason to be bothered by what they'd done than I did, and yet that kind of thing—immorality, if that's what it was—always bugged him.

"Well if Mary votes for Mary and I vote for Mary," Carson said, "then she goes." He looked at me and was clearly looking for some kind of gratitude in my eyes, but everything about him seemed different now that the potential for more was gone. And what did that say about me? That my judgment of a person could be so clouded by romantic interest? A few hours ago I'd wanted to spend my life—or at least the summer—with him and now I didn't even want him on our team?

"Fine," Winter said. "Mary goes."

We had all pretty much devoured our food, and it was Winter who said, "The more pressing question is who's going to ask for a crown?"

I said, "I'll do it," and went up to the guy working the register and said, "Oh, hey"—super casual-like— "can I get a crown?"

The response, "What's it worth to you?" brought him into focus. He was maybe—I was terrible at this—twenty-five? And just a little bit overweight, like puffed up, and he was sweating a little too much.

"I'm sorry," I said, and I turned to my teammates to see their reaction but they hadn't heard so I turned back. "What did you say?"

He looked right at me. "You're like the fifth kid to come in here and ask for a crown tonight. So I'm wondering, how much is it worth to you?"

I didn't entirely understand. "Did people bribe you or something?"

"Not yet," he said. "But there's only one crown left and I feel a certain obligation to make sure it goes to the right person."

"Not yet?!" I repeated loudly, and my friends looked over. "He's fishing for a payoff," I explained.

"Not worth it!" Patrick shouted out, and went back to collecting our trash on a tray. But Carson was up with long fingers on his wallet, coming to my side.

"What's it worth to you?" he said, and something about the whole package of Carson—with his hipster T-shirt and trendy sneakers and hair—must have really irked the guy because he said, "More money than a guy like you could ever give me."

"Woah," Carson said. "You're kidding, right?" which seemed to me to be the exact wrong thing to say, though I couldn't be sure I didn't say it myself—or had I only thought it?—just a few seconds ago.

"This is your big play?" Carson said. "Your big power trip of the day?" He actually fanned the money in his wallet. "How much are we talking?"

"Come on, guys," Patrick said as he slid our trash off a stack of our trays and handed me the rest of my fries in a bag, which I was happy to take both because I was still hungry and because it was nice of him to deliver them to me and that meant something at this stage of things. "It's not worth it."

But it is worth it, I thought.

We were there.

The *crown* was there.

There was just this one guy standing in our way.

I wanted Carson to just put his wallet away and stop acting so clueless and for Patrick to just go out and wait in the car and not be so rigid for once in his life and I wanted, mostly, for Winter to try to charm the guy or something. But right then Winter was engaged only in the process of sucking her chocolate milk shake out of its tall cup.

"Seriously," Carson said. "How much are we talking?"

The guy said, "Give it up, dude," and Carson said, "What's that supposed to mean?"

The guy shook his head and said, "You'd never understand."

"Listen," I said finally, "you've picked the exact wrong

171

team to withhold the crown from. I mean, this guy—look at him."

I indicated Patrick. "He's wearing *suspenders* and knee-highs and got one question wrong on the SAT. He got into Harvard next year, but he can only go if he gets one of a gazillion scholarships he applied for because his parents don't get what a big deal it is."

I turned to Winter. "And this one. Her name's *Winter*. Can you imagine the torture of going through life with the name Winter? Imagine the teasing. The *brrrrrr* whenever she walks by. And her mother spends so much time watching crap TV like the *Real Housewives of New Jersey* that Winter here is pretty much her little sister's stand-in mother, though she works really really hard to make sure no one ever knows that's the case."

I turned, finally, to Carson. "And this guy, he looks like the exact kind of guy you'd hate, but he hardly ever sees his parents and it seeps into everything he does. They bought him that ridiculous car out there, but they weren't even home to give it to him; and he'd probably give it back if it meant his parents were home to see him in the school play and not vacationing in the South of France *without him*."

Returning my gaze to the Burger King guy, I said, "And one of our original teammates is in the hospital with a broken wrist because some of the jock assholes doing the same scavenger hunt tonight never stop dogging him about being gay."

I had to stop to breathe, felt like my brain was swelling inside my head.

"If you want to withhold the crown you withhold it from *them* if they come in here tonight. Because they are going to take one look at you, working here, and figure your whole life is a waste and not think for a second that maybe you can play the guitar really well or do the Sunday *Times* crossword puzzle in an hour or whatever. *We* get that there's more to your life than this."

But when I looked at my teammates for confirmation they were just standing there, staring at me. I took their expressions in, trying to determine which one of them was less mad, and said, "What?" to the group. "It's true!"

"What about you," the guy said. "Why should I give it to *you*?"

I had to breathe, had to think.

What was there to say that could be said?

Because I broke my best friend's heart tonight? Because my other best friend betrayed me? Because the guy I've spent years pining for likes her and not me? I couldn't say any of that, not with them all standing there. I felt my shoulders sink when I said, "Because the King of the Assholes got into Georgetown and I didn't."

The guy took a beat and said, "I believe that's what they call a first-world problem."

"What's *that* mean?" I asked, but the guy just pushed the crown across the counter and walked away toward a long row of flame broilers. I took the crown and walked out and the others followed.

When we went to get into the car, Carson pointed to a small stuffed Winnie-the-Pooh on the dashboard of a car whose driver-side window had been left half open. "Isn't Winnie-the-Pooh on the list?" he said.

"Dude," Patrick said. "We're not stealing somebody's Pooh."

There was no sign of the car's owner.

Patrick added, "We're not stealing anything else tonight. That was the deal."

I didn't remember making any such deal but then again, it was sort of unspoken. We hadn't stolen anything yet that couldn't be returned and I wasn't keen on the idea of starting now. Though Pooh was worth a solid 40 points.

"I made no such deal," Carson said, just as a man approached the car. Carson nodded at the dash and said, "How much for Pooh?"

The guy said, "How much you offering?" He smiled. "I mean, this ain't no ordinary Pooh. This Pooh is straight from Disney World, man."

Carson studied the Pooh doll, which was covered in dust and looked seriously inbred, off-market. "Five bucks?"

"Ten," the guy said, and Carson said, "Fine," and slid a bill out of his wallet.

The guy reached in through the open window to fetch the doll and handed Carson the Pooh and in a minute we were off again, into the night—windows down—with Pooh sitting on the dashboard looking sad and somehow ominous. I wished Carson had thought to just walk away, or charm the guy out of his Pooh. Money made it, what was the word, *dirty*?

After I added up all our new points—we were at 2535—I realized it had been a while since I had heard from Dez, so I texted him: WHAT'S "FIRST WORLD PROBLEM" MEAN?

Right away, my phone lit, and a bunch of texts came through:

LIKE IF YOUR CAVIAR IS EXPIRED.

OR YOU BROKE A HEEL ON YOUR JIMMY CHOOS

OR HAVE TO WAIT TWO HOURS FOR YOUR LIMO

Then after a pause, he sent this: WHY?

I didn't have the energy to reply properly so just wrote, WILL EXPLAIN LATER. MRI NEWS?

He said, STILL WAITING.

A text from the Yeti came right on its heels.

It was the text I had been waiting for all night.

Patrick and the others had gotten it, too, and Patrick read it aloud: "If the lake in the sky has been visited by you/ you've scored yourself a massive clue/just show us the clipper ship's principal namesake/and three hundred points will be yours to take."

"I have no idea what that means," Carson said, and "Me neither"s filled the car.

Patrick said, "God, the poetry just gets worse."

At Patrick's we all went in to the living room and Patrick announced our arrival, our time line—we had to be back in the car in fifteen minutes tops—then told his folks why we were all there. For a copy of his cousin's wedding invitation [80], the Boba Fett action figure [35], the item made of red glass [25], the Superman comic book [50], the Ping-Pong paddle [20], the fan with the remote [40 plus 20], and screwdriver [40].

"That's it?" his mother said, so he handed his mom the list.

"So, how are we doing?" Patrick's father came into the room. "You guys going to take home the Yeti?" He went over to Patrick's mom, stood behind her on the sofa, and started rubbing her shoulders and something about the whole scene made me uncomfortable. There was music playing, and both of Patrick's parents had wine glasses, and were wearing fuzzy slippers—yes, in June!—and if I wasn't careful I could see Patrick's future, the whole of it.

Blissful domestic life.

Me not a part of it.

Why *wasn't* I in love with him? Would that make things easier?

Carson said, "We've got about twenty-five hundred points but we have no idea how anyone else is doing right now. Still, only six teams left and we are clearly the overachievers of the bunch."

"It's looking promising," Patrick said, just as his mother said, "Skinny-dipping?" and raised an eyebrow. Then, suddenly distracted, she said, "Oh! Mary! Prom picture!" She pointed across the room.

Winter was closest to it, a framed photo on a glass table by the front door, and she picked it up to study it. Across the room I could see that Patrick had his arm around me, in my shimmery purple dress, a dress I had loved but which was now burdened with weird memories. Patrick's mom said, "Such a handsome couple," and I wanted to tell her to get her priorities in order and to worry less about a prom picture and more about finding money to send her son to Harvard!

"Mom," Patrick said.

"Well, it's true," his mom said, looking at me sort of wistfully.

"That's my cue," Patrick said, then he headed for the stairs and started to climb two steps at a time.

I said, "We'll all come," and we followed Patrick up the stairs to his room, where he was already looking for the Superman comic book.

"Here," he said to me, and gave me a box of comics, then he put another in front of Winter and another in front of Carson. "They used to be more organized but they got messed up. Any Superman you see was from my uncle's collection and is definitely older than two thousand."

I sat on the bed, flipping through comics, and thought about all the times I'd hung out with Patrick in this room over the last few years—all the movies watched and conversations had surrounded by baseball cards and weird trophies and medals and guitars and keyboards. What if, after tonight's declarations and my unimpressive response, Patrick never got on board with the whole friends thing again? What if we all came home for Thanksgiving come fall and he didn't want to see me? Like, ever?

"Patrick!" His mother's voice came up the stairs. "There's a tent in the attic."

Set up camp somewhere uncampy.

"Somebody come help me," Patrick said, and since Winter jumped up and said, "I'll come," it was obvious to me she didn't want to be alone with Carson.

That left me and him alone with the comic books, which seemed strange, neither of us being that into comics.

"What are uncampy places?" I said.

"I don't know," Carson said. "A rooftop."

"Nah," I said. "People love camping out on their roofs. Maybe someplace indoors," I said. "The mall?"

"Mall's going to be closed by the time we get to it," he said, then we were quiet for a minute, until he said, "Just because they're not around a lot and have money doesn't make them bad people."

It took me a second to realize what he was talking about. I said, "I didn't mean anything by it."

"Even if you didn't, I just wanted to say it. Being rich doesn't make them bad. It doesn't make me bad either. It doesn't define who I am or what my life is going to be like."

"I know," I said, but I had to work to hide the fact that I wasn't so sure. And why had I aspired to vacation in Italy with Carson and to become a staple at places like Mohonk if I thought there *was* something wrong with being wealthy enough to do all that? And how was it possible to aspire to all that and also to aspire to, well, not saving the world, exactly, but *serving*? Why did I want *any* of what I wanted and why did I want it so badly?

"What's going on with you and Patrick tonight?" Carson asked, then, but I didn't want to tell him and was saved by the image of Superman. I pulled the comic book out of the box and checked the date on the cover and said, "Got it!" then stood.

"He told you, didn't he?"

And my mind went to the top secret of the night, to his kissing Winter. "No," I said. "I told him."

"Wait," Carson said. "Told him what?

"What are we talking about?" I asked.

"That he's in love with you," he said.

"Oh," I said. "No." Then, "I mean, yes. He told me."

"And?" He looked at me hopefully and it pained me that he didn't know, would probably never know, how much space in my mind and heart he'd occupied for the past two years, the hours wasted fantasizing, dreaming, planning, scheming. Or maybe one day he would. Maybe we'd sit at a table together at a reunion twenty years from now at the Shalimar and reminisce about scav hunt and from the comfort of my happy life I'd be able to say, "You know. I always had a thing for you," and he'd cock his head and say, "Really? I had no idea," and we'd laugh about it.

"I just don't feel that way about him," I said finally.

"Well, that's too bad," he said, and I managed only, "Yeah."

"I'm jealous, you know." He sat on the bed. "Of what you and Patrick have."

"What do we have?" I asked.

"You know," Carson said. "It's big, your friendship. It's more than friendship, even if you don't want it to be." He smiled a little bit then said, "He would follow you to the ends of the earth."

"I know that," I said, feeling awful that the sentiment made me so uncomfortable. "But I don't want him to. I want to go there myself."

He shrugged. "Sounds lonely."

I said, "Not to me."

Winter and Patrick came back and we went downstairs and said good-bye to Patrick's parents—they'd filled a small box with more stuff from the list, including a Bundt pan [30], a completed crossword from yesterday's paper [75], a can of tuna [3], a picture frame [5], a teapot [30], a bobby pin [30]—then left.

In the car we set out for the meet-up at Rainey, and we all agreed that the others would go by the Cupcake Corral's Dumpster while I was at the park and also try really really hard to figure out the Flying Cloud clue while finding an uncampy place to pitch a tent.

DON'T BE LATE, said a text from the Yeti. And Carson seemed to drive faster.

"We should talk about this meet-up," Patrick said, turning to me.

"What's there to talk about?" I asked.

"What kind of information are you looking for?" Carson said, nodding into the rearview. "What are you willing to divulge? That kind of thing."

I thought for a moment. "Well, I'm looking for anything having to do with the Flying Cloud clue for starters."

"What else?" Carson asked.

"I have no idea," I said, and by this point we'd arrived at the park and the clock on my phone read 8:59. "I think I'm going to have to just wing it."

The gate to Rainey Park was open and I heard far-off voices.

"Wish me luck," I said, and I stepped out into the night.

13

PEOPLE MOSTLY WENT TO RAINEY PARK, UNDER
the bridge, to make out. I'd come here with David Fielder
once during our brief junior-year romance and then never
again with smooching on the agenda. But we had all come
here just to hang out a lot of times over the years and to look
at the city, whose skyline you could just about see off to the
south. Tonight it twinkled like a promise in a clear black sky.
This was where we'd come earlier this year, after our last big
band championship, which we'd lost. It was the place where
Dez, who'd had some beers that night, though no one could
quite figure out where, said that he wanted, more than anything, to walk over the bridge. To just leave Oyster Point and
go to college in the city, where maybe people were different.
But he also said that he was afraid that if he set out to cross
the bridge, he might not make it to the other end without
giving in to the temptation to just jump and be done with it.

"I'm gonna do it," he'd said, standing at the foot of the
pedestrian path across the bridge. "I'm gonna walk over it
and see what happens and if I jump then whatever, right?"

And we'd all pulled him back and he'd sobered up and
that had been that.

We *had* to win. Not for me, but for Dez.

Of course Barbone was there. They'd hardly send Chrissie or Allison or Smitty. But for some reason, the sight of him standing there in the park, without any of the members of his posse, caught me off guard. He was the enemy, and here he was, laughing and yapping. It made me feel a little bit angry and a little bit pathetic at the same time that I despised him so much, and that he seemed to see me as nothing but a nuisance.

Tom Reilly was there, and Kerri Conlon, and Matt Horohoe was representing The Matts. Last but not least, Jill was there, flipping her curls around by Tom.

I should've walked right over to her and apologized for being a jerk at the hay bales. She was my friend. She'd been there that night with Dez, had helped keep him off the bridge. But I felt complicit in Winter's behavior, guilty. Not because Winter was one of my best friends, but because I couldn't be sure I wouldn't have done the same thing if given the chance.

Leticia Farrice and Lucas and the other two judges walked into the park then, with a case of Red Bull, and that brought the total of people there to ten. Something about it felt like a scene from a movie but not a teen movie. More of a heist movie, with an unlikely mix of people being assembled for some complicated bank robbery or hijacking.

The Oyster Point Ten.

Lucas said, "Hey, I was hoping you'd be here," and handed me a Red Bull.

"Why?" I asked. "Did you find her?"

"No," he said. "Sorry. How's it going?"

"Good," I said, a little bit startled by how comfortable he seemed around me and me him. We barely knew each other.

"I mean, the hunt is going good. But I am so screwed if I don't find that statue."

"It'll turn up," he said. "We'll find it."

I nodded and hoped he was right.

You would think that a bunch of teenagers who'd been through all of high school—and in most cases grade school—together, and so had survived puberty and sex ed and the SATs and, well, everything together, would have some kind of stronger, invisible bond, but I felt nothing but awkwardness around most of these people and couldn't imagine ever wanting to show up for a reunion—not in five years, ten, or twenty—not even if it did mean the chance to confess my old crush to Carson.

I was going to head for Jill, but she was talking to Tom, which reminded me that Jill had had a whole other life before Carson, before us. Tom seemed pretty focused on her right now, so maybe there was something to that, and maybe that would somehow let Winter off the hook. If Jill was so quick to move on then would it be okay if Carson did, too?

"So how are you guys doing?" Kerri Conlon asked me, and I turned. We'd had a bunch of classes together over the years, but I couldn't be sure we'd ever spoken one-on-one and now that made me sad.

"Pretty good, I think," I said, trying to remember my goals as laid out by my team. "Did you guys leave town at all?"

"No," Kerri said. "Were we supposed to?"

"Oh, I don't think so," I said. "Just making sure."

Kerri said, "We're mostly focusing on getting stuff and doing stuff, and not spending too much time on all the stuff that's more mysterious or whatever."

"Good strategy," I said, sipping my drink, which was

somehow almost already half gone. "Us, too. What about a Mary on the Half Shell?" I asked, because why not.

Kerri shook her head. "I don't even know what that *is*."

It had to be Barbone. He knew we had the statue. He'd been pissed about the Home Depot thing. It was the only thing that made sense. Unless it really was Jill. And let's face it, I'd been sort of an asshole.

I decided to walk over to her and get it over with. "I'm sorry," I said, "about the hay thing."

"I just don't get you sometimes," she said.

"Join the club," I muttered.

"Did those guys tell you what they did? About prom?" She had this look of defiance, of being wronged, in her eyes that gave her a different sort of confidence.

I just nodded.

"The whole thing is unbelievable to me," she said. "What did you even say when they told you?"

"What's there to say?" I said. "I said it was a shitty thing to do."

"I can't believe you let him join your team," she said.

"I didn't know what he'd done when he joined us," I said. "But even if I had, I mean . . . I'm not sure what I'm supposed to do. He's our friend."

"Is he really?" she asked.

"Of course he is," I said. We were at an impasse. The drawing of this conversation would have a line drawn smack down the middle.

"Please tell me the truth." I sounded weary. "Did you take the Mary statue? Because I was a jerk to you?"

"No, Mary," she said, weary in a different way, like sick of me. "I didn't."

I looked over toward the others, wondered if they were

exchanging valuable hunt information while we wasted time on my own pursuit. "I think it's Barbone," I said. "But he says he didn't take it either."

Jill looked his way, too. "He's not all bad, you know."

"You can't be serious."

Barbone chose that moment to shotgun a Red Bull then crush the can on a wooden picnic table.

"I'm just saying," Jill said, "he has his moments."

"I'll be on the lookout for one of those," I said.

"He saw Carson and Winter," she said, then. "At prom."

I was confused for a minute.

Jill said, "He's the only one who had the guts to tell me."

"I didn't know anything," I said, and I felt like explaining more but confessing my longstanding crush on her ex-boyfriend didn't seem like the best idea.

"Would you have told me if you did?" Jill asked, and then Leticia said, "Can I have your attention?" and everyone stopped talking. Lucas gave me a raised eyebrows look and then came over and took my empty Red Bull and handed me a new one. "Thanks," I said.

"No problem," he said, and I took a swig.

"Okay," Leticia said. "Here's where things get interesting. Raise your hand if you shaved Bob's balls."

Barbone and Tom Reilly and Kerri Conlon all raised their hands.

"Who's Bob?" I whispered to Lucas.

"The bull in Matador Park," he whispered back.

"Ah," I said softly. How did none of us *know* that?

"Who stole something from Mr. Gatti?" Leticia asked, and I raised my hand, along with Barbone and Kerri. "What was it?" Leticia looked at me.

"Garbage can," I said.

She looked at Barbone, who said, "Birdhouse."

Then at Kerri, who said, "Flamingo."

"Excellent," Leticia said. Then Lucas cut in and said, "Speaking of lawn ornaments, who got a Mary on the Half Shell?"

I waited with bated breath but only Barbone raised a hand. Lucas looked at me and mouthed, "Sorry."

"Who has more than two thousand points right now?" Leticia asked. And I scoffed for a moment, because we were already at 3018, but then everyone else's hands went up, too.

"We've only had one Lloyd Dobler so far," Leticia said, and Barbone said, "Awesome."

Some murmured groans rose up from the group.

Then Leticia said, "So if anyone wants to give Lloyd Barbone here a run for his money, you better get busy."

"Who went to Mohonk?" Leticia asked, and only Barbone, Jill, and I raised our hands.

"Good work," Leticia said.

"Who has more than *three thousand* points right now?" Leticia asked, and this time only myself, Barbone, and Tom Reilly raised hands.

"Very impressive," Leticia said. "Anybody gone skinny-dipping yet? We haven't gotten any pics."

Barbone said, "Not yet, but you're welcome to come with, Teesh."

"No thanks," Leticia said to him. She turned to the group. "All right. We just really wanted you all to get a sense of your competition going into the final hours of the hunt. Remember, one a.m. on the dot. No exceptions. And don't forget about Special Points. So good luck and get going."

Lucas approached me again and said, sheepishly, "So about Grace?"

Ugh. So he *did* like her.

"What about her?"

"She's sort of drunk," he said, and I said, "She does that."

I shook my head. I could hardly do anything about it.

"I'll keep an eye on her," he said, and I said, "Thanks."

Barbone found me near the playground on my way out of the park. "How's Daphne, by the way? Still licking his wounds?"

"How do you get to be like you?" I snapped, without realizing I was going to. I guess the Red Bull had me all hyped up. "How do you get to be so *mean*?"

Barbone said, "Let she who is without sin cast the first stone," and I said, "What on earth are you talking about?"

Barbone? Quoting scripture? Please!

I texted my team: COME SAVE ME.

Barbone just shook his head at me and I said, "Just give me back the statue, Jake. My aunt bought it in Europe during World War Two and it's really important to my family. I'll give you stuff worth the points you'd get for the statue. It's not about points, I just need it back."

He looked at me dead on and I noticed, for the first time, that his eyes were blue. "Listen, Mary. I didn't know the statue was brought back from Europe during World War Two. But I'll tell you one thing: if I had something like that in my family and I knew how valuable it was, I sure as hell wouldn't take it for some stupid scavenger hunt."

And that, of all things, shut me up. Because was that how low I'd sunk? I'd done something so awful that not even *Jake Barbone* would do it?

He left me there to deal with myself.

Standing outside and waiting for my team to pick me up, I listened as Kerri told Tom about how her team had gone to some inflatable rat outside the Crowne Plaza and put an ax and a two-by-four in front of him. "I don't get it," Tom said.

Neither did I.

"The rat's picketing or something. And you're supposed to 'put him to work,' so we made him a carpenter, or whatever."

I caught the end of a sentence that Matt was saying to Leticia that ended with the words "Robert's Cove," which I knew to be a dilapidated mansion on the waterfront.

Crowne Plaza.

Robert's Cove.

Carson's car rounded the corner then, windows open and bassline booming loudly, but got stuck at the red light at the corner. And as I looked deeply at that red light—saw the way it was composed not just of one light but of many—I thought, *Let she who is without sin . . .* and remembered something.

Fifth grade. End of the year. We had yearbooks. And Barbone wrote in mine: *You're the prettiest girl in the fifth grade.* Then a graduation party. Mine. My backyard. Our mothers talking while holding amber beer bottles, and his mother saying how maybe Jake and I would get married one day and my mother putting a fake smile on her face and me, not liking the idea—not liking him—and feeling weird about what he'd written. Then him, coming over and asking me if I wanted to play shuffleboard on the driveway. Me saying, "It's my house, Jake. If I wanted to play shuffle-board I'd play shuffleboard." And him saying, "You don't have to be mean about it," and me saying, "And you don't have to be so ugly."

Carson's car was in front of me and I reached out to pull the shiny handle on the back door, almost needing to steady myself. Maybe Barbone was a sort of monster. But maybe I was, too.

"So?" Patrick said.

Carson asked, "What'd you find out?"

"Someone said something about Robert's Cove," I offered.

"That old mansion on the water?" Winter said.

"What did they say?" Carson asked, turning from the driver's seat.

"I don't know," I said. "Somebody Google it and see if that helps."

"On it," Winter said.

"Put the union rat to work has to do with some inflatable rat in front of the Crowne Plaza outside town and making him look like he has a job of some kind?"

"Jeez," Patrick said. "Who figured that one out?"

"Kerri Conlon," I said. "They made the rat into a carpenter with an ax and a two-by-four."

"Any ideas for what job we could give him?" Carson said, but no one had any.

Winter said, "Robert's Cove is that old mansion on the cliff near the park. It's supposedly haunted. And there's like a cutout of a ghost or something on the stairs."

"Photo of a local ghost," I said.

"Yeah," Patrick said. "It's one of the higher point values left. Eighty."

"Should we go?" I asked

"That place gives me the creeps," Winter said.

"All right, then, so we'll skip it," Patrick said, and everyone looked at him. "I'm being facetious."

"Oh," Winter said.

"Let's do it," I said. We had exactly two and a half hours left to the hunt. It was going to go by faster than I wanted it to and not fast enough at all.

"I'm staying in the car," Winter said.

"Ghosts love cars," Patrick said, then he started making *woo-woo* ghosty sounds.

"Quit it," Winter said.

"What else did you find out?" Carson wanted to know.

I completed my report: "Only Barbone's and Jill's teams have been to Mohonk. Or at least that's all I can confirm. They pretty much all shaved the bull's balls in Matador Park. Apparently the bull is Bob."

"Aw, crap," Carson said. "I *knew* that."

"Oh, and Barbone did the Lloyd Dobler thing so if nobody else does, he gets those points."

"Ugh!" Patrick groaned. "*Barbone*? Doing Lloyd Dobler? It's just wrong on so many levels."

"We can still do it," Winter said, and I had an image of Patrick standing in front of the judges, with some melodramatic song blaring from a boom box over his head, his trench coat flapping in the wind. *Say Anything* was another movie we'd watched together, Patrick and I, and the *I gave her my heart; she gave me a pen* line was suddenly resonating like never before. I didn't think I could bear the boom box scene with Patrick in it.

"We don't have time," I said. "It's not a guarantee of points."

"You don't think I'd make a better Lloyd Dobler than Jake Barbone?"

"I'm just saying, there's no guarantee."

"Fine, Mary."

"Don't do that," I snapped. "I hate when you do that."

"When I do what?"

"When you talk to me like I'm a child you're placating," I said.

"When have I ever done that?"

I felt like there were a million times, but of course couldn't think of one right then.

"Is a bug up your ass on the list?" Carson said, pointing to our master copy. "Because I think we have a few right here in the car."

A sort of shocked silence fell over us before Patrick said, "Must be nice to be you."

"As a matter of fact it is!" Carson said, then there was another long silence, and I spotted the carton of six red velvet cupcakes [30] my team had gotten in my absence, on the backseat beside me. They were bit worse for wear, sort of smudged against the clear plastic of the case. I pressed my face against the car window in sympathy.

"What else did you find out, Mary?" Carson said finally.

"I don't know." I pulled away from the window and noted a smudge on it left by my face before adding the cupcakes to the total for 3048.

"That may have been it," I said, then I added, "Nobody admitted to having Eleanor's statue."

"That's it?" Patrick said. "Robert's Cove and union rat?"

"And that everyone has more than two thousand but only us and Barbone and Tom Reilly have more than three thousand and that only Barbone and Jill have been to Mohonk. And that Bob is the bull. That's a lot!" I stiffened. "Like you could have done better!"

"Probably!"

"Well, what have you all been doing that's so great?" I snapped. "Did you figure out the Flying Cloud clue?" I saw the tent still in its bag. "Did you even pitch the tent?"

"I had to climb into a Dumpster for those cupcakes," Winter said.

Carson made a sharp turn and I said, "What are you doing?"

"We're going to my house," he answered. "We're going to hard-boil an egg and cook a singular piece of spaghetti and stage Gumhenge and make a martini and get naked and wet and hope that everyone's attitudes improve after that."

"You know what would improve my attitude?" Patrick said, and Carson said, "What?"

And then Patrick took the Pooh doll off the dashboard and threw it out the window.

"Patrick!" I shouted. "That was forty points!"

So we were back to 3008.

"What the hell!" Winter said.

"Whatever makes you feel better, dude," Carson said.

And I turned and watched Pooh roll across the street and land in the lane of oncoming traffic, where a car ran over him like he wasn't even there.

CARSON'S HOUSE WAS THE NICEST OF ANYONE'S
we knew. It was newer, bigger, and had better stuff—everything from the flat panels on the walls right down to the toilet paper and the contents of the fridge. Over the years we'd come here as a group a lot—after band practice, mostly—and raided the endless stash of awesome snacks and cool sodas, then retired either to the pool or the rec room downstairs—there was a pool table!—to play dumb games, like the Name Game or Truth or Dare.

Winter had wisely grabbed two swimsuits from her house and tossed them into the bag of loot we'd compiled there and now offered one to me, so we could at least get in the pool without having to get our underwear soaked again. It wasn't the sort of swimsuit I'd ever wear myself, though—too pink, too polka-dotty—and once I put it on I felt all sorts of self-conscious.

Barbone had had a crush on me once. How could I have forgotten that?

I was about to get naked in close proximity to Patrick *and* Carson. How had I, good girl extraordinaire, gotten myself into this situation?

Winter, who had been changing in the adjoining bathroom, appeared at the door and my phone, resting on the bed, buzzed. A text from the Yeti said, IF YOU'RE STUMPED AND NEED HELP GETTING OVER THE HUMP, THERE IS AN ITEM ON LIST TWO THAT MAY HELP YOU FIGURE OUT WHAT TO DO.

"UGH!" I moaned. "The clues are only getting me more confused now."

Carson's voice rose up from the main hall. "We don't have all night!"

We bundled up our clothes in a pile on the bed and walked out to meet our fate. Carson was at the bottom of the stairs in a swimsuit and tee and led us out to the yard where Patrick was sitting on the diving board with his legs dangling over. Just like that he slipped into the water with a splash that felt too loud. The yard's far edges were lit by golden gas lamp–style torches and cushy patio furniture sat just beside the pool under tea lights with dragonfly cutouts strung from the branch of one weeping willow to a shadowy oak. Even the stone path under my bare feet felt posh.

"All right," Carson said. "I thought we needed to just take a break from the driving around and sniping and just chill and, you know, purge the bugs up our asses." He made a big sweep with his arm. "Everybody in the pool."

"You're not worried about the bugs coming out of our asses and clogging the filter?" Patrick asked, while I studied the pool's stone edges, the way its figure-eight shape seemed so perfect, so elegant.

"If that should happen," Carson said, "we'll deal."

"Fine by me," Winter said, her swimsuit black and sleek and super flattering and somehow totally right for Carson's backyard. She went over to the diving board and did a near-perfect dive, resurfacing slick like a seal, like she was already some expert trainer at SeaWorld.

"Your turn, Mary," Carson said, and I saw myself as if on-screen, in some lame horror movie, where some malicious predator hid behind one of Carson's yard's fancy trees. I cast myself as the girl who was scared of everything, like skinny-dipping and sex and good-byes and ending up alone, but who would eventually, dumbly, follow some mysterious sound into the house or the trees only to be rewarded with a hand over the mouth, a slash of a knife across the throat, or a wallop on the head. Or maybe the movie's hero—would it be Carson or Patrick?—would suddenly be there, ready to save me.

Polka-dot swimsuit or not, this was not that movie. I wouldn't let it be. Because in another movie I was a girl, with a friend named Dez, and we were eight years old and going for our dolphin badges—treading water for five minutes and then going off the high board. In the pinnacle scene, three of the girls in class had already chickened out and when it was my turn to jump, I was thinking of chickening out, too. But then Dez had turned to the boy next to him—a boy whose name I wouldn't have been able to remember for a million dollars—and said, "No way Mary's chickening out." And that had given me the push I'd needed to get up there and jump.

I ran and jumped off the pool's edge, seeing no need for fanfare, and the water felt warm—needlessly warm—and I almost missed the shock of it, the shock of cold I'd been expecting. Was there such a thing as life being *too* cushy?

When I resurfaced, Patrick was waving his swimsuit in the air like a flag and I ducked from the spray of it, and he said, "Let's get this show on the road."

"Ladies," Carson said, with a smile that seemed a little too cocky, a little too amused, but Winter was already taking straps down off her shoulders so I sunk back down into the water and did the same and soon we'd both put our suits on the pool's edge.

"Okay," Carson said, and he snapped a picture of us then put his phone on a lounge chair and jumped in and slipped his own trunks off and hoisted them up onto the diving board while treading water. "Somebody's got to get a picture with me in it," he said.

But I wasn't getting out, not yet, not when it had taken so much mental energy to get in in the first place. Patrick pulled his swim trunks down off the pool's edge, slipped them on underwater, and climbed out, dried his hands on his T-shirt, then took another picture on the phone. "We're good," he said, and Winter and I reached for swimsuits and slipped them into the water and slipped them back on and Carson did the same and we all got out to dry off. But we'd forgotten to bring out towels.

"I'll go grab some," Carson said.

"I've got to pee *really badly*," Winter said, shaking one of her legs, so they both disappeared through the sliding glass doors of the deck, leaving Patrick and me alone, wet and a little bit cold. After a moment of standing on the deck, dripping, I said, "What's taking them so long?"

"I have one guess," Patrick said, and I pretty much ignored him and turned away.

"You're afraid of me now," he said then.

"I am not," I protested.

"You are," he said. "And if you're not, you should be."

Faster than I could process, warm hands—palms— cradled my head and warm lips kissed mine. It was more burst than kiss, like energy being transferred from Patrick to me through sheer force of will—like he was trying to cram every moment we'd ever shared, every secret spilled, every dream revealed, every deep desire admitted to into one grand gesture—and then it was over and he just looked at me and waited and said, "What about now? Do you see what I'm talking about now?"

He was too much.

Overmuch.

But because I loved him, I didn't slap him or say *What the ef, Patrick?* I gave it a moment—gave my lips and my heart and my head and the rest of me, still practically naked, the time to share signals and hormones and impulses and whatever else they shared, and I took my own heart's pulse but still felt nothing.

"I just don't think that's how it works, Patrick," I said sadly, and then Winter appeared at the sliding door, with Carson behind her, and they tossed towels—warm, dry, thick—at me and Patrick before going back inside.

Patrick towel-dried his hair for a minute while I patted down my body, tingling from the pool but not from the kiss, and then he looked at me with this look that just pained me and I realized he felt like I did—my liking Carson was, to him, the same as Carson liking Winter—and I wished we could somehow console each other, except I knew we couldn't. That, for him, I was part of the problem, even if for me, he—my best friend who adored me—was part of the solution.

"Apparently I once told Barbone he was ugly," I said.

"That doesn't sound like you," he said.

"You always think the best of me," I said, squeezing water from my hair. "Even when you shouldn't."

"That's what love is," he said, and he got up and walked inside.

Winter was brushing her hair the in bedroom where we'd changed. She looked confident—older, somehow—when she said, "Patrick looks like somebody died."

"I feel awful," I said. "He kissed me and I felt nothing."

"It's like you said, Mary. You can't control who you like. You can't feel bad about it."

"Well, I do," I said. "I feel bad about a lot of stuff all of a sudden."

"Join the club," Winter said, then she turned away from the mirror to face me. "How was it?" she asked. "Seeing Jill?"

I was pulling my shirt on over my bra and my skin was cold and dry. "Well, she's pissed."

"Well, she should be," Winter said, a little bit too nonchalantly. She was running fingers through her long wet hair. "But she should be pissed at Carson! Not me!" Then, she added, more softly, "Or at least *more* pissed at him."

I just gave her a look. "Apparently it was Barbone who told her."

"Barbone?" Winter's eyes went wide.

"I guess he saw you guys," I said.

"Well, he's got nerve," Winter said.

"I told him he was ugly once," I said. "Like in fifth grade. When he had a crush on me."

"Well, he is ugly," Winter said, and I just looked at her. She said, "Well, so what. It doesn't excuse him."

"Yeah, but it doesn't excuse me, either."

"You were in fifth grade!"

"Still."

My phone, in my bag on the bed, buzzed. It was a text from Dez: BEING DISCHARGED. SPRAIN. PHYSICAL THERAPY. BUT SENDING ME HOME.

I wrote back: HOME OR HUNT?

"Dez is getting out," I said.

"Is he coming back out?" Winter asked.

"Not sure yet," I said, "but we should hurry, just in case."

Downstairs, the boys had put two pots of water on the stove, presumably one for the spaghetti and one to hard-boil an egg. They'd put the words Le Sabre in lights on the Lite-Brite, even though we were in the Lexus now, and texted it to the Yeti.

"Dez may be coming back," I said.

"For real?" Patrick said, turning to me and holding an X-ACTO knife to Barbie's head. "Awesome."

Winter covered her eyes, not wanting to see her Barbie operated on, as Patrick skillfully dug a hole into the doll's brain. I got shivers just thinking of it ever being done to a living person but if it helped brain function, I thought I could probably do with some trepanation myself. This Flying Cloud thing couldn't be all *that* hard.

Carson was studying Barbie. "What's the difference between a scalped Barbie and trepanation Barbie?"

"Six of one, half dozen the other," Patrick said, then he studied the flesh under the flesh he'd removed. "I guess we have to, like, draw a brain in there?"

"Sounds like a plan," I said, and I crossed the room to the boiling water and put spaghetti in one and an egg in the other. "We could've used one pot, you know."

"Oh, whatever." Carson laughed, and he went and opened the door to the huge pantry and pulled out a bag of flour. "Banana bread recipe plus banana bread is on the list, too. I already preheated the oven." He pointed to a recipe box on the counter. "My mom's recipe is in there."

"Your mom bakes?" Patrick asked.

"Yes, Patrick, she bakes."

"No time for baking," I said, "and we already have a recipe."

Carson stood at a computer that was sitting on the kitchen counter and said, "I think there's some website for police sketching. We could do one of Mullin or Gatti or something."

"Oh," Winter said. "Sounds fun. Let me," and she went over to the computer and stood closer to Carson than I'd ever seen her stand before. They were almost cozy and my brain had to work hard to see that as okay.

Then Carson left to get a sock, and to prepare the martini (Alas, no Piña Colada mix.), and also to get the markers and food coloring for the egg decorating. In the meantime, I sat down at the kitchen table and got busy setting up Gumhenge. My hands were shaking but I got it to stand just long enough for a photo, then I set about ticking off our achievements on the master list.

- Gumhenge. [45]
- Trepanation Barbie. [80]
- Police sketch of Mr. Gatti. A rather impressive likeness, I thought. [125]
- Egg decorated for Easter. [75]
- One piece of cooked spaghetti. [20]
- Put your name in lights. [150]
- Sock [1]
- Martini [80]

"And skinny-dipping," Patrick said. "Don't forget skinny-dipping."

- How could I. [200]

We had gotten 776, which meant 3784.

A text from the Yeti said: FIRST TWO TEAMS TO LASER QUEST GET 200 POINTS. BONUS 250 FOR TEAM WITH HIGHEST SCORING PLAYER OVERALL. SEND POINT TOTALS.

Patrick seemed to read and dismiss the text—rightfully so, I admitted, since Laser Quest was just too far—and said, "Oh, so I've been Googling more and there's this weaponized blimp called the *Flying Cloud* that some guy is writing steampunk stories about."

"A blimp?" I asked as I started to gather our things. Carson was pitching the tent in his parents' bedroom.

"Weaponized blimp," Patrick said. "You know, Mary, sometimes you have to scroll down to like the tenth or eleventh hit to get to the good stuff."

"The screen on my phone is small!"

"Scroll, I said!"

"Fine. Sorry. But what does a blimp have to do with anything?" I asked with frustration. "And what's the item on list two that is supposed to help?"

"Well, I don't know . . . yet." Patrick seemed frustrated, too, but for different reasons. "But it's the only thing I see so far that could possibly lead anywhere. Like if we showed the Yeti the specifications. Or tried to make a small one?"

"Awesome," Carson said, returning to the kitchen and showing me the picture of the tent [75, so 3859]. "We should load up and go."

"Go where?" I asked as we collected our stuff.

"We go get a sub," Patrick said. "At Blimpie. For twenty points and maybe a clue as to what the Flying Cloud stuff is all about?"

"You may be on to something," I said, and I smiled and

felt a sort of mental invigoration. We absolutely had to figure this out!

A text came through from Grace: YOU HAVE TWENTY MINUTES TO GET YOUR BUTT HERE BEFORE YOU'RE GROUNDED FOR THE REST OF THE SUMMER. I KNOW ABOUT THE STATUE. LOVE, MOM

"Oh, shit," I said as I carried the Easter egg carefully out to the car.

"What?" Winter asked.

"Either my sister is messing with me or my mother has taken over her phone and now knows that I'm doing the hunt."

"Crap," Carson said, stowing the cocktail shaker in one of the car's cup holders.

"She said I have twenty minutes to get home before I'm grounded for the rest of the summer."

The next text said: I WILL NOT HESITATE TO CALL COPS ON HUNT!

I studied the texts for clues while we got into the car.

It was the YOU'RE that got me. Because Grace was, we'd always joked, *homophonic*. She could never get her sound-alike words—her *yours* and *you'res*—straight. "It's totally my mom," I said. "What am I going to do?"

"You're going to read an awful lot of books this summer," Patrick said, and laughed and everyone else joined in, too.

"It's not funny!" I wailed. "I don't want to go home!"

"We all have to make sacrifices, Mary," Winter said.

"What sacrifices are you making, exactly?" I asked.

"Well, maybe not *all* of us," Winter said. "But even poor Poppy gave up her precious Goldie for the cause." She laughed and the boys laughed again, too, then Winter said, "Speaking of which," and started digging around in the car and then hoisted up the Ziploc, where Goldie's dead body floated on the water's surface line. "Aw, crap," Winter said, and Patrick and Carson laughed again.

But it wasn't funny. None of it was funny.

Back down to 3794.

Dez's message said: COME GET ME!!!!!

"Dez wants to be picked up," I said, then I shook my head and let it all sink in. "I honestly don't believe this."

There was no way around it. Not if I really *really* wanted my team to win—more than I wanted myself to win. Because I could either throw a pity party right then and ruin it all for everyone or I could appreciate that I'd come pretty far, and that I had friends who could finish the job.

I had to go home.

"Fine," I said. "Drop me off."

"Wait. Really?" Winter said.

"It's the only way."

A text from the Yeti said: IT'S ME, LUCAS. DON'T WORRY ABOUT YOUR SIS. I BROUGHT HER HOME.

Oof. What was it with this guy? He was jamming me up left and right!

"I was sort of joking," Winter said.

"I'll try to reason with my mother," I said, trying to be optimistic. "I'll explain about Dez and Barbone. I don't know. And if I can't come back out, you all can pull this off. I know you can. And I deserve whatever I have coming to me for lying and for taking the statue and losing it."

"We don't really have time to drive to your house," Patrick said. "Not if we're going to get Dez and get a Blimpie and still have time to get some more points."

He was right. "Then leave me at the train station," I said. "Or that car service in town."

"You're serious," Carson said.

"We're not putting you on a train," Patrick said. "But car service is okay. If you're sure."

I was surprised by my own resolve, my own lack of tears and self-pity as Carson headed for the car service place. "I'm sure." I turned to Patrick. "You said before that winning tonight wasn't going to change things for Dez, but I feel like it'd change things for me. I thought it only mattered that I won, but it's just as good if you guys can do it. You have to."

"We'll try our best, Shooter," Carson said as he pulled up by a line of cars for hire. And it was Winter who said, "Why do you even call her that? No one else does. Only her parents."

"I don't know," Carson said. "What's the big deal?"

I got out and left them to it.

AND SO I ARRIVED, A SHORT CAR RIDE LATER,
at home. I felt something new looking at the house I'd grown
up in—at the tiny brick stoop and at the honeysuckle bush
climbing the fence and even at the squeaky old gate to the
yard, where the shuffleboard court we'd painted years ago
on the driveway had long since faded. I suddenly knew I
was going to most miss the very place I wanted so much to
escape, even though I was now dreading walking through
its door.

"Go to your room," my mother said flatly, when I walked
into the kitchen, where she was sitting at the table with a
glass of wine. "I'm not ready to deal with you yet."

So I went upstairs and lay down on my bed and felt sorry
for myself a bit, sure, and thought about the guy in Burger
King. I wondered whether he was still there, flipping burgers and dipping fries into sizzling hot oil with metal baskets,
and I felt grateful I wasn't him.

I believe that's what they call a first-world problem.

Getting caught lying to your parents about your whereabouts and sent to your room while your friends were out in
the world doing dumb things definitely qualified, yes.

Going to George Washington University instead of Georgetown—and having it paid for by my great-aunt—definitely qualified.

Losing a treasured family heirloom? Probably, yes.

My phone buzzed. A text from the Yeti. RUMOR HAS IT ONE TEAM HAS AMASSED A WHOPPING 4500 POINTS. ARE YOU STILL IN THE RUNNING OR SHOULD YOU JUST THROW IN THE TOWEL?

Ugh.

Towel already thrown. Mine, anyway.

Over the next hour, reports from my team came in at a rapid clip.

They got Dez.

They got a Blimpie sub [20] but found nothing there to help crack the clue of the Flying Cloud.

They finally stopped at Jungle Golf, which was just closing up for the night, and snapped pictures of themselves with a gorilla, and a giraffe, and an elephant. [75]

They went to Matador Park with a razor and a can of shaving cream and lathered up the bull Bob's balls and then took pictures of Winter—yes, Winter!—"shaving" them. [80]

They stopped by The Pines, where Patrick, in a trench coat, stood holding a boom box over his head, blasting "In Your Eyes" at Leticia Farrice.

They even, thanks to Dez's Googling, learned that there was a stick-your-head-through-it photo opportunity at a bar called Wunderbar, so they went there and snapped a picture of him in front of a cardboard cutout of a body dressed in lederhosen and hoisting a huge mug of beer. [80]

I was missing it all.

4049!

But I'd turned on my computer and spent some time on the George Washington University website, looking at pictures of the Foggy Bottom campus, where my program had its hub, and reading about dorm life and student life and D.C. in general and getting excited about it for real for the first time. Then I Googled "Flying Cloud" again and remembered, this time, to scroll . . . and scroll.

The whole time I listened to some Blue Öyster Cult band songs, like "Godzilla," which I was pretty sure I'd never heard and "Don't Fear the Reaper," which of course I had. I wanted to imprint them in my brain so that every time I heard them I'd remember this night, the best night of my pathetic life.

There was the Wikipedia entry about the clipper ship.

There was the link to the weaponized blimp stories.

There were the charter boats, and the farm in North Carolina.

And there was a link I hadn't seen yet.

To Airstream.

The trailer company. And a trailer called The Flying Cloud.

My mother appeared in the doorway. "I'm not even sure what to do with you."

"I'm sorry," I said. "I shouldn't have lied. I just knew you wouldn't let me go and it felt . . . I don't know . . . important."

"Important enough to break our trust, and to land Dez in the hospital, and to lose Eleanor's statue?!?!"

So Grace had told her everything.

"Well," I said. "That Dez stuff was really the whole reason we even wanted to enter and to win. To show that the good guys could win, even if they've been tortured, like Dez has, since kindergarten. We wanted, I don't know, some kind of victory lap?"

She came forward and sat on the edge of the bed. "Well, you weren't very committed to your cause if you came home just so you're not grounded this summer."

"But you said you'd call the cops!" I said, and as soon as I did I understood that she had no intention of doing so. "And it's a long summer, and apparently I am not the most noble or moral person out there." I shook my head. "But it wasn't even about that. I figured you could ground me anyway. I mean, you still might, right?" I waited but my mother's expression was blank, so I added, "I got tired of lying and of being so afraid of getting caught."

My mother smiled and shook her head.

"What?"

"You are one smooth talker."

"No, I'm not!"

"Yes, you are. You can be very convincing when you want to be. You've always been like that."

"I'm not trying to convince you of anything," I protested.

"I think you are," my mother said. "I think you're going to try to convince me to let you go back out tonight."

I flattened a wrinkle in my bedspread. "Does that mean that's even a possibility?"

My mother sighed. "The statue is a big deal."

I said, only, "I know."

"The money she left you is paying for your college education," she said. "So I'd expect you to have a little bit more respect for—"

"I know!" I shook my head. "I really am grateful to her for that. I wish I could thank her personally. I wish I'd known."

"That would have made her happy," my mother said, then added, "Actually I'm not sure anything would have ever made Eleanor happy." She laughed, and I laughed, too.

She shook her head then. "I honestly can't even begin to explain how angry I am about the statue."

"I going to get it back," I said, though I realized it wasn't looking good. "Or at least I'm going to try. I'll ask around at school next week. I'll talk to the people who ran the hunt. I'll do everything I can!"

My phone buzzed. It was from the Yeti and said: WE ARE HEAR WAITING ALL STATIONERY. ITS NEARING YOU'RE DEADLINE TO SHOW US THAT PRINCIPAL NAMESAKE.

"What now?" my mother said.

"A clue," I said, and I read it again.

So the Yeti and Grace had that in common.

Hear. Here.

Stationary. Stationery.

Your. You're.

Principle. Principal.

"Oh my god," I said.

The school principal is your pal.

Principal namesake.

Barbone. Mullin. Trailer by the river.

"I just figured out the biggest clue," I said, and my mother sighed and got up to leave the room and lingered for a moment in the doorway. "Well, you should at least have a look around the house so this wasn't a complete waste of time," she said.

It took a minute for the meaning of the words to sink in. "For real?"

"For real," she said. "I've never really liked Jake Barbone. But there are conditions."

"Which are?"

"Eleanor's house. It needs to be cleared out for real—*every last knickknack*—before you leave for school, and I expect you to help every weekend and to not complain about it."

"Done," I said. I wanted to hug her. And not for being the kind of mother who was going to let me go back out, but for being the kind who made me come home in the first place.

"All right, then, go. And don't do anything dumb."

"I'm not sure I can guarantee that," I said, because I had a feeling about what we were about to do.

"Well, don't do anything *dangerous*."

"Promise." I nodded. "Can I take the car?"

"Don't push your luck," she said.

Okay, so transportation was going to be a problem, but I took out the list and read through it again, item by item, and then started rushing around the house, collecting the silhouette of my profile done in Disney a bunch of years back [40], a tape dispenser [30], and a 3x5 index card [5], before remembering the piggy bank shaped like an elephant in Grace's room [45]. I knocked on my sister's door and then walked in to find her in bed, watching TV and drinking Gatorade.

"Can I borrow this?" I lifted her elephant bank off her shelf.

Grace sat up in bed then all but shouted, "She's letting you go back?"

I nodded.

"Unbelievable." Grace shook her head. "You get away with murder."

"Oh, give me a break," I said. "If I'd been out at the senior scavenger hunt as a junior and ended up too drunk to get myself home, I'd be grounded for a year. What's your punishment?"

"My punishment is that my head is still attached to my body," she said. "And I have to work extra shifts at the restaurant every Friday and Saturday night until I earn their trust back."

"You were really drunk," I said.

"I know," Grace said. "And I'm already hungover."

I held up the bank again, for emphasis.

"Fine, take it. Go off and have fun while I sit here and suffer."

"Fine," I said. "I will."

I went down the hall for the Advil in the bathroom then went back into Grace's room and tossed the rattling pill bottle across the room and onto the bed. "Thanks," she said, and I called out, "Least I can do," as I rushed down the hall.

Downstairs, I texted Winter: MEET ME AT MULLIN'S HOUSE!

I stopped in the kitchen and packed all the stuff up into a backpack, and decided that asking my mother for a Tiffany Christmas ornament would really be pushing it, and that it wasn't worth the points.

4169 would have to do. For now.

"I'm taking my bike," I said, and my mother said, "Go." She sipped her wine. "Before I change my mind."

16

IT HAD BEEN A WHILE SINCE I'D RIDDEN MY BIKE.
Like I basically hadn't touched it since I got my driver's
license. But riding a bike was like riding a bike and soon I
was heading down my street and around the corner and past
my elementary school and then my middle school. I took the
right on Albourne Avenue, where there was that great hill
to go down. For a second I thought about taking my hands
off the handlebar and doing it like I used to do when I was a
kid—all free-falling—but then thought better of it and held
on extra tight. I'd been given a second chance at this night
and I didn't want to do anything stupid to mess it up.

I wasn't far from Mullin's house now but my legs hurt.
I'd gotten lazy, being driven around by friends and driving whenever my parents would let me. I was arguably out
of shape and I resolved to bike more this summer, and to
see how bike-friendly D.C. would be. I wouldn't have a car
there, wouldn't need one, but a bike could be fun. Already I
could see myself biking past the White House and the Capi-
tol and exploring all the embassies scattered around Foggy
Bottom. Maybe even biking somewhere to meet Lucas? Like
maybe Arlington, where I'd show him Eleanor's grave and

tell him about how the grateful nation speech had reduced me to a puddle.

I'd gotten a text but I ignored it until I had arrived at my destination and there it was, right in front of me.

In Principal Mullin's driveway.

A Flying Cloud.

"Holy shit," I whispered.

The text from Winter said: OK. WHY????

I texted her back: MULLIN'S RV IS A FLYING CLOUD.

It was silver and shiny under the light that hung just above the garage door—like a big, bulbous beer can without a label. I tried to picture Mullin driving it, down the coast to Florida or out west toward the Grand Canyon. I imagined him in plaid shorts and some kind of hunting hat, running out of gas on some deserted stretch of land.

For a second I was sort of disappointed that all those clues had led us here, to Mullin's. But it also seemed, some-how, fitting.

Winter wrote: !!!!!!!!!!!!!!!!

Then, ON OUR WAY.

I pushed my bike down the road a bit to the nearby bus stop and sat and waited. I was pretty well hidden, so when, a few minutes later, Jake Barbone's car announced its arrival with loud music blaring through open windows, I was able to stay out of sight.

Superfast, I texted Winter to say: WAIT FOR ME TO TEXT YOU. BARBONE HERE NOW. AM HIDING. I left my bike in the bus shelter and snuck into the neighboring yard and watched from behind a line of trees as they got out of the car.

"Dude," Smitty said to Barbone. "You were totally right."

"Told you," Barbone said. "Mullin road-tripped to

213

playoffs in this thing and got so drunk he had to sleep in it in the field parking lot."

"Ugh," Allison said. "I'll never forget it."

"What a pathetic bastard," Barbone said.

That, at least, we agreed upon.

I couldn't believe it had come down to this. Of all the teams I thought would figure this one out, Barbone's wasn't one of them. But then I'd hardly imagined Barbone to be the kind of guy who would tell Jill about Carson's stepping out on her, either. I didn't know him any better than he knew me.

"So what do we do, just take a picture?" Smitty asked.

"Yup!" Barbone said. "Everybody huddle together and say cheese."

"Cheese!" the girls said.

"Hey, should we ask Mullin to pose?" Barbone asked. "For special points?"

"He'd shut down the hunt, man," Smitty said.

"Please," Barbone said. "He totally knows it's happening. He wished me good luck on Friday."

Allison said, "But he'd probably get fired or something if the picture ever leaked out."

"Probably," Barbone said, then: "Dudes! Hundred bucks says we're the only people who got this one. I mean, Tom Reilly and those guys? They didn't even make it to Mohonk so don't even have all the clues to fit together. Kerri Conlon? No way they're even bothering with the brainteaser stuff. The Matts? Probably stoned."

"What about Glee Club?" Chrissie asked, and I braced myself.

Barbone laughed and said, "They're so out of their league it's pathetic. Glee Club was born to lose."

"Let's roll," he said then. "How many points do we have again?"

"With the three hundred for this, we've got 4820," Smitty said.

They got back into their car and the engine started and I ducked farther into the trees out of sight as they passed, feeling like I'd been kicked in the gut.

4820 to our 4169.

Which would be 4469 in a second, once we took a picture of the Flying Cloud, but still. That was 350 points!

COAST IS CLEAR, I texted Winter. Then I pulled my bike back out of the shrubs and thought, *It can not go down like this.*

I was not born to lose.

So we just take a picture? Smitty had asked.

And I got to thinking about that: *Just* a picture? Or *more*?

I heard a car come onto the street then and turned. Carson parked a few houses down and he and the others got out and walked up the block on foot. Except for Dez, who ran to me, and I to him. We embraced, though we had to be careful, with his wrist all bandaged up.

"So, so happy you're here," I said, and he said, "Right back atya, babe."

"So that's the Flying Cloud," Carson said.

I said, "Barbone has three hundred and fifty more points than us."

"Fuuuuuuuuuuuuuudge," Dez groaned.

Then Patrick held out last year's yearbook to me—open to a two-page photo collage where there was a small picture of Mullin standing beside the Flying Cloud. And I had a flash of an image in my head, a split-second fantasy of us winning. And winning big. And of us all celebrating our victory . . . *inside* the Flying Cloud.

So no, not just a picture.

"I have an idea," I said. "Because we don't have time to catch up on points any other way and we can't count on stuff like Mr. Gatti's trash can being the biggest thing or on Pictionary or Lloyd Dobler. We need to do something big. Something unexpected. Something that will totally get us Special Points. And a lot of them."

"We're all ears," Winter said.

"Spit it out," Carson said.

I took a deep breath and let it out. "We have to take the Flying Cloud to The Pines."

"What?!" Patrick said.

"No way," Winter said.

"You're crazy," Carson said.

"It's the only way," I said.

Dez nodded, and a smile spread across his face. "It says *show us* the Flying Cloud."

"Exactly," I said. "So let's do it for real. No picture this time. We *bring it* to them. For all we know, that's the 'marvelous dare' of that clue."

Patrick said, "It's just not possible, Mary."

Winter turned to me and winced. "I think he may be right."

"Barbone was just here," I said, and my voice was shaky. "And he was already acting like they'd won the whole thing, and he said that we'd never win it because we were out of our league. He said we were born to lose."

Dez and Winter were shaking their heads.

"I don't know about you guys," I said. "But I, personally, have never felt more like a winner."

There was a long pause then and I wasn't sure which way it was going to go but then Winter said, "Well, we should at least talk it through."

"We'll need the keys," I said, right away.

"This is crazy," Patrick said, but I was choosing to ignore him.

"We might not actually need to get *in* it," I said. "But the hitch probably has a lock, right?"

"But the *car* needs the other end of the hitch." Winter shook her head. "We're doomed."

"Not necessarily," Dez said, slowly.

"How do you figure?" Carson said.

"Mary," Dez said. "Go take a picture of the hitch and lock, if there is one. Serial number if you can get it."

"Okay," I said. "I'll be right back." I took off toward a line of hedges that ran on the far side of the driveway and started to inch up the driveway toward the Flying Cloud. When it appeared no alarm would go off, no lights or dogs or sirens, I started taking giant steps until I was right up against the Airstream. I reached up to open the door but it was, of course, locked. Peeking out the front edge toward the house and seeing no new activity, I went to the hitch and took a picture of the lock there with my phone. Then I crawled under it and found the serial number on the lock and typed it into a memo on my phone. I got up again and hurried back to my friends then showed them the picture.

Carson said, "I have no idea what I'm even looking at."

"It's hard to see," I said, "but there's a padlock with a keyhole and it like holds this pole in there so that you can't hitch it to anything." I turned to Dez and said, "What's the big idea?"

"Back to the car," he said. "The last thing we want to do is get caught before we even do anything."

When we were all back in the car, Dez said, "Okay. Send that stuff to me and I'll text my dad."

"Brilliant," I said.

So I texted him and he texted his dad and we all waited and his phone buzzed and he reported back. "My dad says he sold Mullin the lock. That you absolutely need the key. And that it's *possible* there's another lock in the same set at the store and that it would have the same key, but he's not actually at the store because he had to come to the hospital because of this." He held up his wrist.

Patrick said, "Well, we're hardly going to break into Mullin's house. Especially with him home."

"No," I said, thinking back to that day in the office with Mullin, to him having no idea who I was, and an idea started to form. "It's better that he's home."

"Why?" Dez asked.

"You tell me," I said as the plan started to solidify. "What would the world's lamest scavenger hunt team do?"

After a moment, Dez said: "I don't know. Would they knock on his door and ask him for his trailer?"

I smiled. "Something like that, yes!"

"You are a criminal mastermind," Dez said, and I loved him for figuring out what I was thinking.

"I don't get it," Winter said.

I explained: "We go up to Mullin's door and tell him about the hunt. Like we're ratting everybody else out. We play it all straight and earnest, like he should call the cops or something. And while we do one of us slips away and tries to find the keys."

"But what if he does call the cops?" Patrick asked.

"He won't. He wished Barbone good luck on Friday. He already knows about the hunt and hasn't done anything."

Winter said, "But even if we find the key and unlock it, we still need to hitch it to something."

218

Could we rent a truck from Home Depot?

There wasn't time.

There wasn't time to buy a hitch and hook it up to Carson's SUV either.

There was only one solution.

"I hate to have to say it." The air around us felt full, a water balloon ready to explode. "We need Jill. We need Jill's dad's truck."

"Let me think about this," Carson said, sounding panicked.

"There's nothing to think about," I said. "We need help. There's no way the four of us can pull this off. So we need to find Jill and those guys and talk them into joining forces."

"There *has* to be another way," Winter said wearily.

"I'm all ears if there's another way," I said, and Dez said, "She's right. It's the only way."

"I'm texting Jill," I said.

"And saying what?" Carson asked.

"Saying we all need to meet up and talk," I said.

"There's *no way* I'm dealing with her right now," he said.

"That's the spirit," Patrick said wryly.

"I don't know what your issue is tonight," Carson said.

"Oh, my issue is in no way limited to tonight," Patrick said.

"What exactly did I do to you?" Carson asked.

"You didn't do anything to me," Patrick said. "But man up, Carson. The way you think you can solve everything with money and the way you go from girl to girl and how they let you"—he threw a look at Winter—"it just boggles the mind."

"Oh, get off your high horse." Carson's hands were on the steering wheel, gripping it tight. "Like pining for the same girl for your whole life makes you somehow a better person, more noble or something? Snap out of it. She doesn't like you."

"Carson!" Winter shouted.

Patrick got out of the car. "I'm done with this."

I got out and went after him, saying to Dez, "Get her here. And fast."

"But, Mary!" Winter said.

"You're going to have to face her sooner or later," I said, and walked off.

"Patrick!" I called out, and jogged to catch up with him. "Come on! How are you even going to get home from here?"

He stopped and turned and his face was all red from anger and something else and I said, "Please. We're so close."

"To *what*?" He shook his head. "To stealing Mullin's trailer? Who *cares*, Mary?"

"I do," I said. My voice didn't echo exactly, but it seemed to travel and resonate in the night.

"But *why*?" He put his hands on his hips and waited.

I looked around, like the words might be out there for me to pluck from the air. "Because I want to live a little, I don't know! I can't go through my whole life feeling like some second-class citizen or also-ran. And I want to see the looks on all of their faces when we drive back to The Pines with the Flying Cloud trailing behind us."

"That hardly seems an honorable motive," he said.

"Who said anything about honor?" I asked.

He held my gaze. "But why do you even care what they think, any of them?"

"Because I'm *human*!"

But it wasn't even about proving it to Barbone or Mullin anymore. It was about proving it to myself. Because I wasn't going to go very far in life if I wasn't willing to take chances, even stupid ones, sometimes. And if I didn't start owning my own fate now, when would I? Besides, we hadn't come this far to not even bother trying.

"It's a good idea," I said, and it was true I was maybe still convincing myself. "It'll win it for us, I just know it."

We just stood there, the night pulsing around us. And it all felt very dramatic and finite, some kind of turning point in our friendship, like a new beginning or an end. "I love you, too, you know," I said, feeling teary then. "I don't want to lose you."

"You're not going to lose me, Mary," he said sadly. "Where would I go?"

And so there we were, two stick figures so very close together and so far apart.

"Please don't go home," I said. "Not now. I need you here."

"You don't, actually," he said. "You can do it just as easily without me."

"But I *want* you here," I said. "I want to remember this night for the rest of my life and I want to remember you in it, with me all the way."

A car was coming down the street and we both turned. It was Jill.

"You really want to do this?" he asked.

"More than anything I've ever wanted to do before," I said, and it was the exact kind of statement that Patrick would usually challenge, like by saying, "More than you wanted to go to Georgetown?" or "More than you want to stop global warming?" But he didn't say any of those things. He said, "Well, then I guess we better get moving."

"WHAT'S SO IMPORTANT THAT IT CAN'T WAIT?"
Jill said. "And why are we *here*?"

She and Patrick and I were standing beside Carson's car, curbside, while her car idled nearby with Mike and Heather still in it.

"You know the clues about the Flying Cloud?" I asked.

"Yeah."

"It's Principal Mullin's trailer." I pointed. "That's it."

Jill turned.

"And Barbone figured it out and took a picture of it and sent it in and he probably has enough points to win the whole thing. But we came up with this plan. We go to Mullin and act like we're ratting out the hunt, but meanwhile the rest of us—you—are driving away with the Flying Cloud."

Jill actually guffawed. "You want to *steal* it?"

"Borrow," I said. "If we literally *show* the judges the Flying Cloud, they'd have to give us a ton of Special Points."

Jill just looked into the car, where Winter sat entirely still in the backseat, and sighed. "You know," Jill said to her, "I used to like you."

I felt a sort of head-to-toe sting, like a bee had somehow stung my central nervous system. I couldn't imagine how Winter felt, but I looked at her, urged her with my eyes.

"It was a shitty thing I did," she said after a moment. "I know I can't take it back, but I'm sorry."

"I used to want to *be like* you," Jill said to her. "Because I thought you were sort of above all the bullshit at school and that you just seemed real or something. But I don't know." She shook her head and I noticed again how pretty she was, how soft her features were.

"I'm really, really sorry," Winter said.

"Why should I help you all?" Jill asked, but it wasn't exactly a question. "I mean, honestly, right now, I'd rather Barbone win than *him*." She was looking at Carson but it was Dez who said, "You don't mean that."

"I do!" she said.

"I deserve that," Carson said.

Jill let out a "Ha" and said, "Oh, I'm glad you approve of my feelings."

I had a feeling we were going to be here awhile.

"You do deserve it," Dez said to Carson, then he turned to Jill. "But *Barbone*, Jill. I mean, *come on*. Barbone! You know how much he's tortured me. Seriously, if you don't want to help with the Flying Cloud, at least just take all our stuff and you can win it that way."

I wanted to object, but it was a good idea.

"Isn't that cheating?" Jill asked, and looked at me.

"Probably." I shrugged. "I don't know. I just know that I'd hate for what Carson did—what Carson and Winter did—to ruin this night, when we don't even know how much of this any of us is even going to remember twenty or fifty years from now. I mean, I might not even be able to remember your last name when I'm old and gray and you might forget mine, too. You might forget all about Carson and Winter, or at the very least look back and wonder why you were so mad about it because you didn't even like him near as much as you'll like the next person you meet or the one after that or the one after that."

I was running out of air.

"But I think if we took Principal Mullin's Airstream trailer for a joyride and won the hunt, we'd remember that for sure."

"I don't know," Jill said, and she looked over at the Flying Cloud and a smile started to tug at her features. "Maybe you're right."

"So what are you saying?" I asked. "Because time's running out."

"I'm saying that *you*"—she looked at Carson—"are a prick." She looked at Winter—"And you better watch out for the next girl he's got his eye on." She looked at Dez and then at me, "And you guys are going to owe me big-time."

I nodded and said, "We need your dad's truck."

"Yeah, I get it," Jill said. "I get that I'm being used."

"It's not like that!"

"I know," Jill said. "I'm kidding. Mostly."

"But will he just let you take it?" I asked.

"No." Jill shrugged. "They'll ground me for sure. But it'll be worth it. And they usually get sick of having me moping around all the time after a few weeks anyway. I am a highly skilled moper. Let me go tell Heather and Mike."

So we all put our heads together to hash out details of the plan.

"You think it'll work?" Winter asked me as we sprung into action a few minutes later.

"I honestly have no idea," I said, and it felt good, the thrill of not knowing.

We moved all of Jill's team's loot into Carson's car since she was going to have to leave her car at home and he suggested he take it all to The Pines, to put it in Patrick's car, so there'd be more room for passengers. That seemed a sort of unnecessary step to me, but he seemed pretty determined and it was true we'd have a hard time all fitting. Of course, we wouldn't need to if we had the Flying Cloud with us but as Patrick had said, it was a pretty big *if*.

I offered to go with Jill, Mike, and Heather to get her father's truck while Winter, Dez, and Patrick kept an eye on the Flying Cloud. Heather and Mike seemed happy to have me and happy to be along for the ride, having a final adventure of the night. I wondered why everything on my team had felt so *complicated*, but I wouldn't have wanted it any other way.

A few houses down from Jill's, she stopped the car and told us to get out and wait on the corner out of sight, then said, "Wish me luck." She drove the rest of the way and pulled into her house's driveway. Heather and Mike and I watched as she disappeared inside, and saw a light go on in the kitchen.

Heather said, "You're seriously crazy, you know."

"Certifiable," Mike said.

"Well then what are you two doing going along with me?" I asked, and they both smiled and shrugged.

Superfast, Jill was outside again, then starting up the

truck, and backing down the driveway. She almost took out the mailbox by the road on her way out but didn't. Heather and I then squeezed into the cab and Mike hopped in the back and Jill drove back to Mullin's.

It was all happening so smoothly, so quickly, that it seemed inevitable something was about to go wrong. And yet, as we all gathered near the hedges in front of Mullin's house, there seemed to be nothing in our way.

"We ready to do this?" I asked, and it felt like that imaginary bee that had stung me had left my whole body buzzing.

"Ready," Dez said.

Then Patrick said, "So say we all," and he smiled with excitement and I felt sure things were going to be okay again for all of us, that maybe they already were.

Winter and I headed up the path to Mullin's house with Patrick and Dez behind us and rang the bell. Jill, Mike, Heather, and designated driver Carson—who had more experience driving trucks than any of us—were waiting just beyond the shrubs for the signal to back the truck into the driveway, which would be a light turned on in the downstairs bathroom, whose window faced the driveway. Then turned off again, then on again.

"You know your part?" I elbowed Winter.

"I think I won't have to try too hard," Winter said.

The door opened.

"Hello," Mullin said, looking a touch confused. "Can I help you?"

"Can we come in?" Winter asked. "It's important."

"Do I know you?" he asked me, and I was about to say a

simple, "No, but I go to your school," but he said, "Oh, right. Georgetown."

"Right," I said, and my face felt hot. "Please can we come in?"

"At . . ."—he turned to look at a wall clock—"twelve thirty on a Saturday night?"

"Principal Mullin," Patrick said, sounding all grown up. "It's about a rather urgent matter."

"Well come on, then," Mullin said, stepping back to let the four of us in. "If you must."

Inside, Winter and the boys sat with the principal in his living room and I excused myself to the bathroom as Winter started babbling. She was good at babbling. This was the perfect role for her and she stole the scene, just being herself. I heard her telling the principal about the hunt and how Dez's dad told them it was going on because all these kids were in Home Depot buying random things. And how we were just hanging out in the park after a movie, minding our own business when Dave Fitzgerald got into a fight with Dez and broke his wrist.

"Wait," Mullin said. "Dave Fitzgerald did that?"

"Yes, sir," Dez said.

I stopped, and waited, breath bated, for some big reaction from Mullin, like maybe a declaration he'd expel Fitz on Monday, but none came.

"Anyway," Winter said, but I couldn't afford to listen anymore. I found the bathroom, turned on the light and the fan, then turned the light off, then on again, and closed the door without going in.

I went down the hall to the kitchen and started looking for keys in drawers or on hooks in cabinets, but there were none.

I opened the door that led to the garage and saw some keys on the wall there, and saw two on an Airstream keychain. Snatching them, I went back to the kitchen, passed the keys out the window to Mike, who'd been told to wait right there. I went back down the hall, opened the bathroom door, flushed the toilet, and rejoined the others in the living room.

"Anyway," Patrick was saying, "we just thought we should let you know."

"Yeah, thanks," Mullin said. "I'll take this all under advisement."

I looked around at my friends and we all nodded and I said, "Well, then I guess we'll be on our way."

Mullin went to get up to show us the door but Patrick said, "No need to get up, sir."

Mullin's attention was already back on the television. A baseball game on the West Coast. Bottom of the 13th. "Oh, right," he said, waving us off. "Great. Thanks."

We went outside and walked calmly down the now-empty drive and down the street to where the Flying Cloud was hitched to Jill's dad's truck. When we were close, we took off into a run, with laughter chasing us then catching up and overtaking us. Mike was in the truck with Carson—whose car we were abandoning there—and Jill and Heather were in the Flying Cloud so the rest of us climbed up and in. We were all sort of winded and quiet until Patrick started laughing and said, "We are in some serious trouble now."

Carson took a wide turn and we all swayed and grabbed onto things and then settled into seats and couches. It was all so organized in there—not an inch was wasted—that it made me feel even more scattered, more all over the map, and I liked it, that feeling of not being so neat all the time. Then my eyes fell on a photograph—of Mullin and a woman, perhaps a wife or girlfriend, smiling in front of a waterfall. I'd never thought much about the fact that Mullin was "single" but whoever she was must have left him or died and I had a thought about life being messy, no matter who you were.

I felt tears forming—I couldn't believe we'd actually pulled it off—and thought that yes, this was worth risking being grounded all summer.

This was worth whatever punishment was coming from Mullin, though I had a feeling he wasn't going to do much of anything.

What was there left to do, really, with so few days left to the school year? And what could he do to me—to any of us—that really mattered in the grand scheme of things?

Jill was looking at her watch as the Flying Cloud took another floaty turn. "We're not going to make it."

"We have to," I said, but as soon as I said it I realized I wasn't sure it was true. Not anymore. I said, "Or maybe we don't."

Because we'd already won, hadn't we?

I sure felt we had.

And what did it matter, the official title? The Yeti? The stamp of approval from Barbone? Who really cared what any of those guys thought anyway? The thought of having to see them all again actually ruined the mood.

But we were almost there.

So close.

I could see the entrance to The Pines—the shadowy trees,

and the dim glow of the lights of school beyond it. Carson was heading there at full tilt.

HOLD UP, said the text I sent to Carson, and the Flying Cloud stopped and everyone said, "What's going on?" and then Carson and Mike came over to the trailer door and I hung out of it and I pointed to The Pines and said, "Look at it over there."

Loud music blared and a few tipsy girls were shouting and dancing on cars.

I said, "I couldn't think of any place I would rather be less."

"You want to just give up?" Jill asked. *"Now?"*

"It's not giving up," I said, shaking my head. "We do what we came to do and show them the Flying Cloud but we don't stop. We do a drive-by—a victory lap—and we take this trailer and hit the road and see where we land."

"Works for me," Dez said, then he pulled as many of us as he could into a hug and said, "You turned out to be the best scav hunt team ever."

Patrick said, "Let's get this show on the road," and we all laughed.

So Carson got back into the truck and drove us into The Pines and it all seemed to happen in slow motion, then.

I saw the heads start to turn our way, one by one, like some kind of stadium wave.

And then jaws started dropping and mouths starting moving and saying this:

Holy.

Shit.

And then the look on Barbone's face, the look of defeat and disappointment, and maybe something else, too, though it was hard to say what it was. Was he maybe even a little bit impressed?

And then our circle of the lot was complete, and I saw Leticia Farrice and the Yeti and Lucas Wells—smiling and nodding at me—and I waved a small wave and we headed back out into the night.

I plopped down on one of the small benchlike sofas, between Patrick and Dez—Winter and Mike and Heather had settled at the kitchen table—and everything felt right.

We parked the trailer by the beach end of Rainey Park where there was a small stretch of sand down by the river.

"I don't want things to always be so weird between us," I said to Patrick, when we sat down apart from the others on the sand, with the lights from inside the Flying Cloud illuminating the scene.

"They won't be," he said. "I promise. I will get over it. Over you, I mean."

"Good," I said. "Because there are plenty of girls out there who'd kill to be with you."

"Mary, stop," he said.

"No, it's—"

"Just stop, okay?" He sounded serious that time.

"Okay," I said, then really fast—before he could even interrupt—I said, "You'll find some Harvard hottie and you'll never think about me that way again."

"Let's not get ahead of ourselves," Patrick said, and I just nodded.

"What do you think you'll remember most about all this?" I asked him. "About high school?"

I knew now that I'd remember Patrick's bubble-fro in front of the Shalimar, and Dez singing "The Rose" on the way to Mohonk, and the look on Winter's face when we stole

Poppy's Pillow Pet from right under her sleeping head. I'd remember all of it any time I ever saw an umlaut or heard the Blue Öyster Cult on the radio and I'd sing along to "Don't Fear the Reaper," and mean it.

"I don't know," he said. "Because the stuff I want to remember most is stuff I'm not leaving behind, if that makes any sense."

It didn't. "Not really."

"I won't have to remember *you*, for example, because you're still going to be a part of my life. A different part, for sure, but we'll e-mail and see each other on break and during summers." He thought some more. "I'll miss band, I guess, and probably other stuff that I don't even know I'm going to miss until I go away and realize I do."

Carson was laughing loudly at something Winter was doing and I said, "What about Carson?"

"Yeah," Patrick said reluctantly. "I'm going to miss Carson. I mean, I love the guy, warts and all. But I don't know…"

"What?" I thought I knew what he meant. "You can say it."

"I think there's another best friend—best guy friend—in my future. Probably a lot of them."

"Life is long," I said, and I nodded.

Patrick said, "If you're lucky."

There was talk then, about taking one joy ride or road trip, before returning the Flying Cloud to its rightful owner. But where to go? We couldn't decide. It didn't seem worth the bother. This spot was pretty nice, felt pretty perfect. Especially when Dez popped inside the Flying Cloud with his iPod and started blasting music.

"I'm sort of dying to know who they gave the Yeti to," Dez said when he came back out and sat beside me on the sand.

I just shrugged.

He elbowed me. "Oh, now all of a sudden you don't care?"

"This is better than winning." I nodded. "We won the moral victory."

"You think?" he said.

"I think," I said, and marveled at how much had happened since Hayhenge, since the origami sheep in the ER waiting room. "Hey, why were you mad today? At the hospital. When we were talking about Barbone and Fitz?"

Dez scooped some sand and let it run through his fingers and I realized we never got a chance to play Pictionary with the judges, never got to draw a picture of a duck or a fire hydrant or a moat. He said, "It just seemed like you all thought Barbone was some hero by not messing with the fag."

"But you know we don't feel that way," I said, maybe a little too knee-jerk before I let the accusation set in.

"But how *do* you feel?" he said wearily. "I mean, none of you really messes with me either. I'm handled with kid gloves. Nobody has ever even asked me if I'm gay."

"Well, *are* you?"

"It's so like you to miss the point, Mary." He sighed. "Of course I am. I mean, have you *met me*? I just mean we've never talked about it. Why is that?"

"I figured you'd talk about it if you wanted to."

"I want to!"

"Well, why didn't you say so?"

"I don't know." He was wiping sand from his palms now. "Why should I have to? Why doesn't it just happen naturally? We talk about everyone else's lame crushes ad nauseam, but never mine."

"Who is it?" I pinched his leg through his jeans. "Tell me!"

"Not now, you idiot." He swatted my hand away. "But let's say we open a dialogue."

"I love it when you talk diplomat," I said, and felt pretty sure that Dez could walk right over the bridge and to the city tonight, without a second thought. Then I saw a figure walking down the beach.

Leticia Farrice.

"What's she doing here?" I said. And then I saw what she was carrying, what she had hugged to her chest in front of her.

The Yeti.

And Lucas Wells was walking behind her.

They came to where we were sitting, and Leticia put the Yeti down so that its feet sunk slightly into the sand. He looked for a second like he might make a break for it—maybe dive into the water and swim to the opposite shore—but of course I was probably projecting.

"Well played," Leticia said. "Here you go."

"But we didn't turn up for judging," I said, bewildered.

"Well, you pulled into the parking lot, so technically you did," Lucas said. "And I happen to be the Head Judge for Special Points and I awarded you enough of them to win the whole thing."

"How'd that go over?" Patrick asked.

Leticia said, "Honestly, I think they were all too impressed to even try to argue."

"It was pretty unbelievable," Lucas said.

"Well you were the ones who came up with the marvelous dare," I said.

"We only called it that because it rhymed," Lucas said. "It never occurred to us someone would read that much into it."

Dez and I exchanged a look and then we high-fived each other and started laughing. "How did you even find us?" I asked.

Lucas said, "I just asked myself where I'd go if I'd pulled off something so entirely awesome."

"I've got to take off," Leticia said. "But you guys are in charge of the hunt next year. It's more work than you think it is, so get started early."

I had already started. I was going to have a ton of fun messing with the minds of Grace and her classmates come next June. Though it was going to take a while to come up with something like the Flying Cloud and all the requisite clues.

"I also have this for you," Lucas said, and he unzipped his backpack and pulled out Mary on the Half Shell.

"Oh my God." I rushed forward to hug her—and him, which felt weird and also not weird at all. "Where *was* she?"

"It was the strangest thing," he said. "It was like one minute she wasn't there and the next she was. Right next to the Yeti in The Pines. Like someone wanted her to be found. Maybe an hour ago."

He seemed to be looking over my shoulder and I turned and saw Carson there, looking caught out.

"It was *you*?" I said.

"I can explain," he said.

"This ought to be good," Dez said.

"Privately," Carson said, and I wasn't sure whether I even cared what he had to say because I was so relieved to have Mary back, but I followed him down to the water anyway.

"What the hell?" I said, still clutching Mary, whose robe was coarse like fine sandpaper.

He took a deep breath then let it out and said, "Sometimes you just seem a little harsh and sort of, I don't know, judgmental."

I was about to say, "You're joking, right?" but I bit my tongue and waited.

"And I knew you were going to make me feel bad about what Winter and I had done and make *her* feel bad and I guess I just wanted to get back at you somehow. But I didn't know about the history of the statue and I wanted to come clean earlier but then I knew how it would look."

"It looks pretty bad," I said.

"Well, I'm not perfect," he said, and I said, "Well neither am I, but still."

"I know," he said. "I'm sorry, okay?"

"Yeah, I guess," I said, but I knew something had changed that wouldn't change back.

We took a bunch of pictures, then, of us with the Yeti on the beach. And the Yeti and Mary on the Half Shell together.

And the Yeti and Mary in the Flying Cloud.

And then each of us leaning against the Flying Cloud.

I made sure that there were some of Winter and me— not joined at the hip, but close—and then some of all four of us, the original Also-Rans, and then a picture with just me and Patrick and the Yeti. I thought for a minute— hard—about taking a picture of Winter and Carson, but somehow, it didn't seem necessary, or even right. I had a feeling that they weren't even going to get together in any real way.

It didn't matter.

Carson wasn't the one for me. He wasn't even the one for right now. My life would hopefully have its great love story but this wasn't it. It would happen in D.C. in the next four years or it would happen in Africa, if I ever got there, or in Sienna or, for all I knew, Kentucky or Timbuktu.

Life *was* long.

And people only really had great love affairs in high school in the movies. And maybe during world wars. But this was not a movie and not a war, even if it sometimes felt that way. It was only high school and it was almost over with anyway.

"So why'd he do it?" Winter asked me, in a quiet moment.

"He said he knew I was going to make you feel bad for cheating, and that he was going to give it back, but then it sort of escalated."

Winter nodded. "That's pretty lame."

"Yeah," I said, and I felt bad for her that her great romance wasn't so great either, then I nudged her. "I think this would have been a pretty okay teen comedy in the end."

"Comedy?" Winter laughed. "More like tragedy!"

"Tragedy *is* comedy," I said. "Didn't someone famous say that once?"

"Um." Winter laughed. "Like I'd know."

"I think you wouldn't have minded playing yourself in this movie, though." I nudged her.

"I don't know," Winter said. "I had to do nudity and Dumpster dive. And the pay's crap."

Then she said, "Hey, you never wrote the first paragraph of a novel about Oyster Point High."

"No," I said. "I never did." But I had a feeling I could

now, if I had to, and that it might even be a funny, happy novel, and not one about a school better left at the bottom of the ocean.

It was time. Patrick got in to drive Jill's dad's truck this time and everyone else got into the Airstream and that didn't seem right so I hopped out and went to ride with Patrick.

"Hey, you," he said, when I got in.

"You looked lonely," I said.

"Always," he said.

So we drove, and the sky above us was so black it was almost blue again, and with the windows down you could hear the stereo from the Flying Cloud blasting, *There goes Tokyo! Go! Go! Godzilla!*

"We need to make a stop," I said, and I pulled Mary out of my bag and held her up.

"Gotcha," Patrick said, and he drove on, with what felt like new purpose.

When we stopped out front of Eleanor's house, I got out and some of the others were hanging out of the Flying Cloud, saying "What's going on?"

"Returning Mary to her rightful place," I said, and I went to work on the weeds, clearing the path between the garden's edge and the statue's stone perch. I'd come back tomorrow to finish the job, but for now it was much improved. I took Mary and sat her back down on the stone and made the sign of the cross and tried to pray, but it was hard with the Blue Öyster Cult singing, *History shows again and again how nature points up the folly of man/Godzilla!*

Barbone would be in school on Monday. The last week of school. And he'd have something to say about Dez, the Yeti, the Flying Cloud, all of it. And then he'd be at Georgetown in a few months and I might bump into him on the streets one day. I'd try to hold my head high and accept that Georgetown was his fate and mine was mine.

And Lucas's, too, which was sort of fun to think about. He'd texted me after he'd gone home, saying: SEE YOU SOON?

Something didn't feel quite right about just leaving Mary there all alone, though.

"Hey, guys?" I called out to the Flying Cloud. A few faces came to the window again. "What do you say we give the Yeti a new home right here?" I nodded toward the grotto.

"Yeti on the Half Shell?" Dez asked.

"Yeah," I said. "Mary needs a friend."

"Sure," Dez said. "Why not?"

So they passed the Yeti through the window—it was heavier than I expected—and I put it in Eleanor's garden and stepped back. It looked just right, like it might stop running after all.

I saluted the Yeti and gave Mary a pat on the head and got back into the truck with Patrick. Then we set out to find out whether Mullin had even missed the Flying Cloud, whether we'd be arrested or expelled, and whether any of us cared.

ACKNOWLEDGMENTS

If I ever do a scavenger hunt again, I want these fine people on my team:

Sara Zarr, who would try to talk me out of shaving my eyebrows.

Siobhan Vivian, who would hand me the razor.

David Dunton at Harvey Klinger Agency, who would gamely act as if I looked great without eyebrows.

Nick, who would tell me that I did not.

Bob, who would lend me an eyebrow pencil.

Julie Strauss-Gabel, who would suggest that I re-do the pencil-eyebrows a few times, to get them just right.

And Liza Kaplan, who would quietly ride shotgun through all this eyebrow nonsense and somehow get us enough points to qualify.

Copious special points to Ellie, and to the makers of the University of Chicago Scavenger Hunt lists of years past, for providing inspiration.